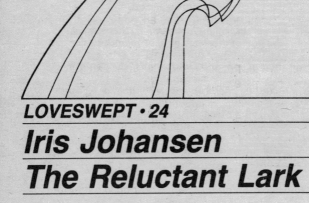

LOVESWEPT · 24

Iris Johansen
The Reluctant Lark

🐓 **BANTAM BOOKS**
NEW YORK · TORONTO · LONDON · SYDNEY · AUCKLAND

THE RELUCTANT LARK

A Bantam Book / November 1983

LOVESWEPT® and the wave device are registered trademarks of Bantam Books, a division of Bantam Doubleday Dell Publishing Group, Inc. Registered in U.S. Patent and Trademark Office and elsewhere.

ISBN 0-553-21625-2

Published simultaneously in the United States and Canada

Bantam Books are published by Bantam Books, a division of Bantam Doubleday Dell Publishing Group, Inc. Its trademark, consisting of the words "Bantam Books" and the portrayal of a rooster, is Registered in U.S. Patent and Trademark Office and in other countries. Marca Registrada. Bantam Books, 666 Fifth Avenue, New York, New York 10103.

PRINTED IN THE UNITED STATES OF AMERICA

OPM   11   10   9   8   7   6   5   4   3   2

Sheena could see his smoky breath on the still cold air above her, as he said, "You're like a fine-boned kitten, all softness and silk. And you're all mine, aren't you?"

She raised her head to protest, to tell him no, that she was no one's possession. But she met the golden intensity of his eyes and the words died away without being spoken. There was no arrogant superiority, no smug triumph on his face at that moment. There was only an exultant joyousness and a depth of tenderness that seemed incredible.

"Just as I'm completely yours," Rand said huskily, and slowly bent his head to take her lips. Sheena felt her throat tighten with unshed tears at the sheer beauty of the moment. His lips were warm and coaxing as they brushed across her throat to rest against the pulse beat in the soft hollow. "You're beginning to realize that now, aren't you, love?" he murmured. "You're beginning to know that I'd never take anything from you without giving a more than even exchange." His warm lips were on hers once more, and she could feel her heart stop in her throat at the glowing tenderness of his embrace. "Give to me," he urged softly. "Open to me, dove. Let me love you, and I promise that you'll never want to fly away again. Can't you feel that you've come home at last?"

WHAT ARE *LOVESWEPT* ROMANCES?

They are stories of true romance and touching emotion. We believe those two very important ingredients are constants in our highly sensual and very believable stories in the *LOVESWEPT* line. Our goal is to give you, the reader, stories of consistently high quality that may sometimes make you laugh, sometimes make you cry, but are always fresh and creative and contain many delightful surprises within their pages.

Most romance fans read an enormous number of books. Those they truly love, they keep. Others may be traded with friends and soon forgotten. We hope that each *LOVESWEPT* romance will be a treasure—a "keeper." We will always try to publish

LOVE STORIES YOU'LL NEVER FORGET
BY AUTHORS YOU'LL ALWAYS REMEMBER

The Editors

One

"You were absolutely terrific!" James O'Daniels said jubilantly. "You had them in the palm of your hand!"

Sheena Reardon stood quietly in the wings as her uncle, Donal O'Shea, gently patted her face dry with a towel and Sean Reilly stood waiting with a glass of water to soothe her throat. Mr. O'Daniels was right, she thought indifferently, as the roaring applause continued even though she had walked off the stage two minutes earlier. The concert had gone exceptionally well, and this New York audience was tremendously responsive despite what she'd heard of their blasé sophistication.

"The reviews are sure to be raves tomorrow," the concert promoter continued enthusiastically. "You really blew their minds, and you didn't even have your best song on the program."

Sheena's hand tightened involuntarily on the glass. Then she took a sip of water and handed the glass back to Sean. She smiled with an effort and accepted her guitar from a waiting stagehand. "I'm glad you were pleased, Mr. O'Daniels."

As she turned to go to her dressing room, her uncle touched her shoulder caressingly. "All right, darlin'?" he asked gently, his gray eyes troubled.

She kept the smile fixed firmly on her face as she nodded. "I'm fine," she said huskily. She would be, she assured herself. She was always exhausted after a concert. This odd lethargy would disappear after a good night's rest.

Donal O'Shea fell into step beside her as she strode swiftly to her dressing room. "He's right you know," he said quietly. "They were with you all the way. You wrung the hearts out of them, love."

"That's nice, Uncle Donal," Sheena said listlessly. "Mr. O'Daniels seemed very happy about it all."

She opened the door to her dressing room, and he followed her in and closed the door behind him. "You could appear a little more enthusiastic," he said reprovingly. "James O'Daniels is a very important man in concert circles, and he's done a great deal for you. He's even arranged this party tonight to introduce you to some very influential people." He crossed to the easy chair in the corner of the room and dropped into it, watching her with narrowed eyes as she seated herself at the mirror and began to apply cream to remove the heavy stage makeup from her face. "I think it might be best if you wear the black gown tonight instead of the gray. We want you to make the proper dramatic impact."

"All right," she murmured. It didn't really matter what she wore. All her clothing was either black, gray, or white. Her uncle was convinced that it was important to maintain her image as "Ireland's Mournful Dove" in her private life as well as on the stage, and he'd seen to it that her entire wardrobe echoed the theme. Though she'd noticed that black did make her appear a trifle gaunt of late.

She was thinner than when the tour had started, she realized, gazing at herself in the mirror. The thinness of her face made her black eyes look even more enormous in their extravagant frame of long, dark lashes and threw her high cheekbones into startling prominence. Uncle Donal had always teased her about her "foreign" look, saying that she looked more like a wicked Spanish señorita than a good sturdy Irish colleen. Her full lower lip lent a curiously passionate look to her face, and her glossy dark hair was allowed to fall halfway down her back in a tangle of gypsylike curls.

She made a face. "I wish I could just forget about the party and go back to the hotel." She sighed. "I'm so tired."

"I know you are, darlin'," Donal said soothingly. "It's been a long, hard tour, and you've been an angel from heaven. I promise you that when we return to Dublin I'll arrange for you to have a nice, long rest."

There was a wry smile on Sheena's face as she watched him stand up and walk toward the door. Uncle Donal meant well, she knew, but he had been promising her that rest for almost three months now. He simply forgot that everyone did not possess his own driving energy.

Even his appearance was almost overpoweringly aggressive, she thought affectionately. He was only a little above average height, but his square, powerful body and barrel chest had an intimidating strength. Then, too, for a man of fifty-eight, his blunt features were surprisingly youthful, and only a few grizzled gray streaks in his curly brown hair bore testament to his age.

"Sheena, love," he said hesitantly, as he paused by the door, "you're going to do 'Rory's Song' tomorrow night."

She inhaled sharply, and she could feel the color drain from her face. "Do I have to?" she asked faintly.

Donal O'Shea nodded, his gray eyes warmly sympathetic. "I promised O'Daniels that you'd do it. It's a great drawing card. Even more so since you haven't done it for the entire American tour."

She moistened her lips nervously. "I know, Uncle Donal, but . . ."

There was a thread of steel beneath Donal O'Shea's kindly tone as he said coaxingly, "I know it's difficult for you, love, but you know that it's necessary. We mustn't let them forget about Rory and the way he died, even if it's painful for us to remember. You wouldn't want that, would you, dear?"

Sheena closed her eyes for a moment, experiencing a swift jab of pain at the gentle reproof. Then her lids slowly lifted to reveal tear-bright eyes. "No, I wouldn't want that," she said huskily. The door closed softly behind him.

Sheena sat quite still and drew a deep breath, fighting for composure. How foolish to allow herself to become so upset. She knew that she couldn't avoid including "Rory's Song" in her repertoire indefinitely. She had been lucky that her uncle had not deemed it necessary before this. She knew that he tried to spare her the ordeal as much as possible, but there were times when he had to insist on the song. It wouldn't be so bad, she assured herself desperately. Her uncle and Sean would be there to offer their usual comfort and support. They were always there when she needed them.

She mustn't think of that now. She automatically plucked out a tissue and began wiping the cream from her face. She had O'Daniels's party to get through, and her uncle would be most upset if she didn't say and do the right things. Not that she would hear anything but the gentlest reproach from him. After her parents' death in an automobile accident when she was eleven, he'd been kindness itself, taking her brother, Rory, and her into his home and his life without a thought and lavishing on them a bountiful tenderness. But his care and affection deserved to be returned with equal thoughtfulness.

She searched her mind frantically for a subject to distract her thoughts from the ordeal to come the next night. Then, as if by magic, a bronzed, rugged face and a pair of strange golden eyes appeared on her mental horizon. She stared absently into the mirror, not seeing her own finely drawn face but the bold, masculine features that had been haunting her ceaselessly of late. She felt a tiny frisson of excitement surge through her. Would he be there again tonight?

He *was* there again.

Sheena's eyes had searched the crowded room with an almost compulsive fascination until she spotted the tall, muscular figure leaning with casual grace against the wall on the far side of the room. She didn't know if what she felt was fear or excitement when she finally ascertained that he was indeed present once again.

"I see you've spotted our social lion," Barbara O'Daniels said cheerfully, as she came up behind her. She handed her the cocktail she had wrested from a passing waiter before continuing enthusiastically. "He's really quite something, isn't he? Even if he wasn't such a fabulous catch, he could still put his shoes under my bed anytime."

Sheena felt an obscure sense of shock at the remark from so young a girl as her host's pretty nineteen-year-old daughter. But then she had felt the same discomfort ever since she had arrived in America three months earlier. Young women seemed to grow up very quickly over here, she thought uneasily, or perhaps it was her own sheltered upbringing that led to this conclusion. At any rate, Barbara O'Daniels had been very pleasant to her since she had arrived at this cocktail party, and she had no right to be critical.

"And who is your social lion?" Sheena asked lightly, trying to mask her sudden intense interest in Barbara's answer.

"You mean you don't know?" Barbara asked incredulously, her blue eyes widening. "That's Rand Challon!"

"He's some sort of entertainer?" Sheena inquired,

knowing the answer even before Barbara shook her head. That magnetic, powerful figure possessed a charisma that had no connection with the limelight.

"Good Lord, no!" Barbara said derisively. "He owns practically the whole state of Texas, plus several other parts of the world. He's head of Challon Oil and owns a fabulous ranch called Crescent Creek. The man's a billionaire and one of the most powerful men in the world!"

"Is he Irish-American?" Sheena asked. Everything that the younger girl had told her had just increased her puzzlement.

Barbara shrugged, "Not so far as I know," she answered. "Why?"

Sheena shook her head in bewilderment. "I don't know. I just had an idea I'd seen him before. I thought perhaps he might be a fan of Irish folk music and I might have seen him at one of my concerts or perhaps at one of the parties afterward."

Barbara's eyes widened with curiosity. "Really, where?"

"Chicago," Sheena answered quietly. She wondered if the girl would think she'd gone completely mad if she mentioned that she'd also seen Challon in Miami and San Francisco as well.

"You must be mistaken," Barbara O'Daniels said positively, "I'm sure I'd know if he was interested in folk concerts. Daddy is one of the foremost concert promoters in New York, and I'm certain he would have mentioned it."

"Perhaps you're right," Sheena said slowly. "I must have been mistaken. It was probably someone who resembled him."

"That would be practically impossible," Barbara said, giving Sheena an impish grin. "There's no one who looks like Rand Challon. The man positively oozes sex appeal. Just watch my gorgeous stepmother hanging on his every word."

Sheena noticed for the first time that the woman standing talking to Challon was indeed her hostess,

Bridget O'Daniels, and she could see why Barbara's voice was tinged with cynicism. Bridget O'Daniels's chatter appeared to be electric in vivacity while Challon's response seemed to be amused indulgence.

If Challon was the high-powered tycoon that Barbara described, he must also be something of a sportsman, Sheena decided. In his early thirties, the man's deep tan and muscular body were evidence of a vigorous outdoor life. His thick, curly hair must have been brown at one time, but it was now sun bleached to a tawny shade between gold and bronze. His features were too blunt and rough-hewn for conventional good looks, but they had a power and rugged attraction that was obviously wildly pleasing to the besotted Bridget. The tailoring of his pale beige business suit and vest was both faultless and expensive.

The object of Sheena's curiosity looked up suddenly, as if conscious of her perusal of him, and met her eyes. Sheena felt an electric shock surge through her that was startling in its intensity. His eyes were a clear amber gold and had the piercing hunger of a stalking lion. For a moment she felt absurdly as if she were caught, captured, held in that glance like a helpless gazelle in the paws of the lion of her mental simile.

There was no surprise in his eyes as they held hers. It was almost as if he had been waiting for this moment of realization and recognition. Sheena felt a tingle of fear run down her spine at the bold, possessive sureness in that stare, but for some reason she found it impossible to look away.

Then arching a brow and smiling mockingly, Challon lifted his glass in a silent toast.

Sheena's cheeks burned with embarrassment as she hurriedly looked away from his arrogantly knowing expression. What had possessed her to be caught gawking like a schoolgirl at her first dance? There had been both tolerant amusement and a teasing challenge in that mocking gesture before she forced herself to look away.

It was quite clear that the man was used to the effect that his virile magnetism had on women, she thought vexedly. Well, she would be most careful to keep from increasing that egotistical self-confidence.

Barbara O'Daniels had observed the exchange with bright, curious eyes. "Perhaps he does recognize you," she said. "You know you've really become quite well-known over here since you started touring." Then, realizing that she might have committed a faux pas, she added hurriedly, "not that you weren't already famous, of course. All of Europe knew you as 'Ireland's Mournful Dove.' It's just that Daddy says that a performer can't really consider herself an international star until she's accepted by American audiences."

"I'm sure your father is right," Sheena said soothingly. "I don't see why my uncle would have arranged this tour if he didn't agree with him."

"Thanks heavens you're not one of those temperamental artistic types," Barbara said, breathing a sigh of relief. "Daddy would have been perfectly furious with me if I'd offended you. Tonight's concert was a tremendous success, and the one tomorrow is sure to be a sellout. He thinks you're absolutely super."

"Your father has been very kind to me. I'm glad that I didn't disappoint him."

"No chance," Barbara said. "You're really good. That passionate, husky little voice of yours could be sexy as hell if you'd sing something besides those gloomy tearjerkers." Then, abruptly realizing what she'd said, she grinned sheepishly. "Oh, Lord, I've done it again. I guess you've noticed that diplomacy isn't one of my principal attributes."

"I've noticed," Sheena said, a ghost of a twinkle in her dark eyes.

"It's just that I'm more into rock than folk songs at the moment," Barbara said lamely. She was obviously uncomfortable, and her glance was ricocheting around the room in search of an escape route. Her face lit up as she spied Sean Reilly across the room. "There's that dishy red-haired assistant of your uncle's. I think I'll just go over and extend a little seductive American hospitality." She raised her eyebrows inquiringly. "Unless I'm poaching on your preserves?"

"What?" Sheena was startled. "No, of course not." She had never thought of Sean in that way. He was just her uncle's assistant, an extension of that comforting presence that protected and pampered her. Following Barbara's gaze to the corner of the room where Sean stood chatting with the smooth, easy courtesy that she'd grown accustomed to, she realized that he was very attractive. His auburn hair, bright blue eyes, and tall, sturdy body were doubtlessly very appealing. "We're just friends."

"Good," Barbara said with satisfaction. "Then, if you'll excuse me, a-hunting I will go." She disappeared into the crowd.

Sheena stared after her for a moment, feeling oddly lonely in the crowded and smoky room. It was almost suffocatingly hot, and she was beginning to feel claustrophobic. Surely she'd done her duty for the evening and could go back to the hotel. It seemed that she'd been introduced to hundreds of people, and her smile felt as if it were frozen on her face. She was just making her way across the room to ask Sean if he knew of her uncle's whereabouts, when she felt a hand on her arm.

"Come on, little dove," a deep, masculine voice murmured in her ear. "Let's get the hell out of here!"

She had never heard that voice in her life before, but she didn't have to glance up at that bold, rough-hewn face to realize to whom it belonged. Ignoring her gasp of protest, Challon propelled her across the room toward the french doors that led to the penthouse terrace.

As he opened the door and pushed her out ahead of him, the only protest she could think to utter was a weak "But it's raining outside!"

"Don't worry about it," he said grimly. "You won't melt in the real world, despite what your uncle tells you."

Rand Challon closed the glass doors behind them with a sharp click that had an ominously final sound to it. He then swept her a little to the side, where the overhanging eaves sheltered them from the steadily falling rain.

She looked up at him, trepidation gradually being replaced by indignation. The arrogance of the man, sweeping her from the room like a pirate with booty! "You may enjoy standing in the rain, but I do not, Mr. Challon," she said icily. "If you'll kindly release my arm, I'd like to return to the party."

"The hell you would," he returned with blunt coolness. "I saw your face just now. There's nothing that would please you less than going back to that high-pressured hothouse in there."

"You're very sure of your powers of perception," she said caustically. "What makes you think that you can read a perfect stranger with such ease?"

"Do you know that you have practically no accent at all until something upsets you?" he asked absently. "Though, of course, your mother was American, wasn't she?"

Sheena felt a jolt of surprise, and her eyes widened. "How did you know my mother was American?"

His smile was a flash of warm sunlight in the bronze darkness of his face. "There's not much that I don't know about you, little dove. We're far from being strangers. I think you realized that tonight, didn't you?"

"I don't know what you're talking about," Sheena said, her dark eyes wary.

"I think you do," he said. "I believe you first discovered that I was following you in Miami."

"San Francisco," she corrected, her head whirling in confusion at the bewildering statement. "Following?" she asked faintly. "I thought it a mere coincidence. I had no idea that I had such an ardent fan."

He shook his head. "I was at your first concert in Houston, and I've been at every one since, but I can't say that I'm a fan." He grinned ruefully. "To be honest,

I hate your performances with a passion." His face lit with amusement as she raised her chin haughtily, her dark eyes blazing with outrage and hurt. "Just settle down, little dove," he went on soothingly. "It's simply that I've never believed in attending funerals, even with a lovely thing like you as chief mourner. I have a passion for life and the living, not for death."

"If you're quite finished insulting me, I'll leave you now," Sheena said, her voice shaking with rage. "By the way, Mr. Challon, I couldn't care less what you have a passion for!"

"You will, dove. I assure you that I intend to make you conversant with all of my passions." He smiled gently. "As for leaving me, I'll let you go in a few minutes, at least for a time. I'm not trying to cage you at present, little bird. I just thought that it was time I made my first approach. I could see that you were getting a bit uneasy when you finally realized that I was on your trail."

"You're absolutely crazy," she sputtered. "They ought to lock you up and throw away the key. You can't follow someone around just because it amuses you to do so."

His grin widened in frank enjoyment as he looked down at her furious face. "When you're as rich as I am, you're not called crazy, just eccentric, sweetheart. And you'll find out that I can do pretty well as I please."

"Not with me you can't! Besides, why would anyone want to follow a total stranger around the country?"

He smiled lazily. "I'm tempted to tell you, but I don't think you're ready for it. Let's just say that I'm doing some very important reconnoitering before I launch my offensive. I knew after your second concert that I was going to have a hell of a battle on my hands, and I took pains to make sure that I had all the ammunition needed to fight it."

"Battle?" she asked dazedly. "What battle?"

"Not now, love," he said softly, his eyes glowing amber gold. "You wouldn't understand at the moment." Gently he cupped her cheek in his hard, warm palm.

"Let's just say I'm planning on turning my mournful dove into a lark."

"You're completely mad," she whispered. She was suddenly acutely conscious of Challon's vibrant nearness, the pulse that was beating in his strong bronzed throat, the heady scent of warm male flesh mixed with the clean odor of soap. Standing isolated between the curtain of gently falling rain and the barrier that the glass french doors formed between the two of them and the noisy party a few feet away, it was almost as if they were in a private world of their own.

Sheena shook her head to clear it. Was she as insane as he was? Why was she feeling this melting, boneless warmth in her every limb? Her heart was beating like a trip-hammer for no better reason than that golden, intimate look, which seemed to wrap her tenderly yet securely in its velvet web.

"God, but you're a temptation, sweetheart," Challon said thickly, his eyes accurately reading and interpreting the telltale glow in her jet black eyes. "If I hadn't promised myself that I'd try patience and gentleness first, I'd whisk you out of here and take you home with me."

She could feel her cheeks turn warm, and she looked away hastily. "It might not be entirely your decision to make," she said tartly, lifting her chin haughtily. "I'm not accustomed to letting strange men carry me home like some sort of trophy."

Challon chuckled, his lean cheeks creased with amusement. "Yes, I know, little dove. I'm going to have to exert all my expertise to overcome that convent upbringing."

"How did you . . . ?" she started, then trailed off helplessly. Was there nothing the man didn't know about her?

"Tell me," he asked suddenly, "are you doing 'Rory's Song' tomorrow night?"

She felt a little ripple of shock. "Of course I'm doing it," she said. "Not that it concerns you."

"Everything you do concerns me, Sheena," Challon said quietly. "But I admit that this particular decision comes as no surprise to me. It fits the pattern quite neatly with what I've observed in the past three months. Don't you ever question any edicts issued by your dear uncle? Do you really enjoy being a lovely mindless puppet?"

"Puppet!" she exclaimed, furious. "You have no idea at all of what you're saying. My uncle loves me, and he only does what's best for me."

"Would a man who loves you dress you in mourning black and send you up on stage in front of thousands of people to rip your soul to shreds?" Challon asked grimly.

"It's not like that!"

"Oh, isn't it? Then what is it like, Sheena? Tell me what you feel when you're out there in front of that mob who only want to taste your tears and touch your agony."

Her huge dark eyes misted. "Please," she pleaded huskily. "I don't want to talk about it. Won't you just go away?"

He shook his head, his golden eyes tender. "Never again, little dove. There's always pain before healing; you're wounded, and I want to be there to kiss it better."

"Sheena, what are you doing out here?" Sean Reilly's voice, unusually sharp, cut through that breathlessly intimate moment. He closed the french doors behind him and approached with his usual silent grace. "It's pouring, and you know how bad the dampness is for your throat." He whipped off his tweed jacket and draped it around her solicitously, the movement deftly separating her from Challon.

Challon observed the ploy with lazy amusement. "It's my fault, Reilly," he said mockingly. "I assured her that she wouldn't melt. It seems that I stand corrected."

Reilly shot the older man an annoyed glance before turning to Sheena and smiling. "It's a crazy, wild girl you are," he scolded gently. "Come along inside, and I'll get you a drink to ward off a chill."

"I don't want a drink, Sean," she snapped. "I feel perfectly well."

Reilly gave her a look of stunned surprise, and Challon's sudden laugh had a note of triumph in it that pleased her as little as Sean's gentle coerciveness. "Have you met Mr. Challon, Sean?" she asked briskly, as she took off his tweed jacket and handed it back to him.

There was a flicker in Sean's blue eyes. "Rand Challon?" he asked slowly. Challon nodded curtly. "How is it you know my name, Mr. Challon? I don't believe we met before."

"Mr. Challon doesn't have to rely on such pedestrian things as introductions, Sean," Sheena said tartly. "He merely looks into his crystal ball, and all things are clear to him." She turned and sailed regally through the french doors, followed closely by Reilly. Sheena resisted an impulse to cast a backward glance at Rand Challon. She'd had enough of his mockery and amusement . . . and mysteriousness.

Sean's silky voice was curious as he murmured softly in her ear, "You two were very absorbed when I interrupted you. What were you talking about?"

She shrugged. "Nothing important." Somehow, she didn't want to share those bewildering, intimate moments that she had spent on the terrace with Challon, even with a good friend like Sean. "It seems that Mr. Challon is a bird fancier. We were discussing the relative merits of doves and larks."

Two

"Good God in heaven, you must have lost your wits entirely to even think such a thing," Donal O'Shea barked, his face flushing angrily. "My niece has given her solemn word that she will appear at the benefit concert, and appear she will!"

"I'm sorry you feel that way, Mr. O'Shea," Henry Smythe said a trifle pompously. "I'd hoped to convince you that it was for the good of your country to help Her Majesty's government by cooperating. I've already explained that the NCI is planning to use Miss Reardon's appearance at the concert next month as a persuasive tactic in convincing several wealthy Irish-American industrialists to contribute arms to their organization. Surely you wouldn't want to bear the responsibility of the bloodshed that would result if they succeeded in their aim."

Sheena focused her gaze on the brilliant bulbs that surrounded the mirror of the dressing table and tried to close out the voices of the arguing men around her.

She was so terribly tired, and there was still the concert to endure. She needed time to steel herself for the pain that was to come. Oh, God, why couldn't they just go away? When her uncle had called and asked Sean to bring her to the theater early, she'd had no idea that it was to meet this prim little civil servant with his weird, daft tales. Why couldn't her uncle have handled the matter himself as he usually did?

"Are you accusing my niece and me of belonging to that bloodthirsty bunch of terrorists?" O'Shea asked incredulously, his face becoming even redder with anger.

"Certainly not," Smythe said hurriedly. "You've both been scrupulously investigated, and there's appeared no trace of a connection between you and the group. I merely said that they may be using your niece for their own ends. She's become something of a folk heroine since her brother died a martyr's death at the university. She's gained a tremendous following both in Ireland and Europe with those tragic little folksongs she sings. There's even evidence that they may have spread a special cloak of protection over her activities for a number of years. Perhaps ever since her brother, Rory's, death five years ago. An informant notified us six months ago that word had been passed that the Reardon concerts were sacrosanct to the NCI. No bombings or other terrorist activities were to take place at any function at which she appeared."

"You've the typical blindness of the English," O'Shea retorted. "Did it never occur to you that evil as they are, those rebels are still Irishmen and can be stirred by my niece's songs like any other men?"

"Perhaps we should let your niece decide," Smythe said wearily. "Surely the concern and responsibility are primarily hers." He cast a rather doubtful glance at Sheena's small, indifferent figure sitting in front of the mirror.

"My niece has complete faith in my judgment," O'Shea said sharply. "And I won't have you upsetting her with your foolishness."

"I wouldn't have taken the time to come here tonight if I'd thought I was on a fool's mission, Mr. O'Shea. I believe you owe me the courtesy of at least consulting with Miss Reardon."

Sheena gave a little sigh of resignation and looked away from the mirror. She'd hoped to avoid any direct confrontation with the Englishman and had tried to close herself away from the pain and memories his arrival had generated. She had realized as soon as she'd seen him who he was, even before he'd identified himself. God knows she had talked to enough of his ilk after Rory had died. Smythe was exactly the dapper, graying bureaucrat that her uncle most despised. Now it was clear that he would not go away until she'd added her refusal to her uncle's.

"Mr. Smythe, I don't even know what the NCI is," she said impatiently. "How could they possibly be using me for their own ends?"

Smythe frowned. "You must have read about them in the newspapers, Miss Reardon. The National Coalition for Ireland is the bloodiest terrorist organization in Irish history. Their leaders were originally members of the IRA, but they grew impatient when the IRA efforts failed to free Ireland." He smiled mirthlessly. "The IRA finds them as much a thorn in the flesh as Her Majesty's government does."

"My niece isn't concerned with politics," O'Shea said curtly.

"But it's vitally important—" Smythe started.

"My uncle is quite correct, Mr. Connors. I trust him completely," Sheena interrupted firmly, with just a hint of Irish brogue in her husky voice. "If he says you're mistaken in your belief, then I can't possibly do as you wish." She looked away from him, down at her hands, which were folded on her lap. Now perhaps he'd be satisfied.

Couldn't he see how futile arguing with Donal O'Shea would be? There was a streak of pure iron beneath that bluff kindness and loving protectiveness. He had been both mother and father to her since she and Rory had come to him as two desolate orphans after their parents' death. He had enfolded her in that warm kindliness and given her something to cling to in that sea of loneliness. But she'd always been aware that the strength she clung to could also be an immovable force if challenged. There had been a few times before Rory's death when she'd issued that challenge, but it hadn't seemed worthwhile since that hideous day in Ballycraigh. Nothing had seemed to matter after that.

She could hear them still arguing and exhorting and tried again to close them out, but it was becoming increasingly difficult. Then she heard Sean Reilly enter the conversation, and she breathed a sigh of relief. Sean would smooth over the turbulent waters with his usual easy charm.

"Arguments can be very thirsty work, indeed, gentlemen," Sean Reilly said genially. "Suppose I take Mr. Smythe to the little bar around the corner, Donal? Perhaps you can join us after the concert for further discussion. It's almost time for Sheena to go on."

Smythe gave a glance of grudging approval at the good-looking young man. "Very well," he agreed reluctantly, rising to his feet. Reilly gave him another flashing smile before ushering him, with charming courtesy, out of the dressing room.

Sheena drew a long, quivering sigh of relief as she heard the door close behind them. It was only a moment later that her uncle crossed the room, gently pulled her up into his arms, and rocked her with all the tenderness he had shown her as a small child.

"I knew that idiot would upset you," he said fiercely. "I tried to get him to leave you out of it, but he insisted on seeing you. Blasted bureaucrat!"

"I'm fine, Uncle Donal," she said hurriedly. "It's just that he reminded me of all those other men in their dark business suits and their questions. All those interminable questions."

He stroked her dark hair soothingly. "Forget it all

now, darlin'. I won't let him talk to you again. Haven't I always taken care of my little lass?"

She nodded contentedly, then looked up suddenly, her dark eyes troubled. "There was no truth in it, was there, Uncle Donal? That man was wrong, wasn't he?"

"Of course he was." He tilted her head to look gently into her face. "Now, you must put a smile on that pretty face. It's almost curtain time, *alanna*. You'd best hurry and get dressed."

Sheena drew a deep breath to steady the fluttering in her stomach. It was time. Uncle Donal always put "Rory's Song" last on the program, both for dramatic impact and to make it easier for her. All she had to do was get through the next several minutes. She could do it. She had before.

She walked quietly to the center of the stage and settled herself on her stool. She didn't acknowledge the waves of applause at her reappearance until she was settled with her guitar cradled in her arms. Then she only looked up to announce gravely, " 'Rory's Song.' "

It was enough. The audience quieted immediately after the first excited whisper that swept through the house. Then all their attention was fixed on that fragile, black-gowned figure on stage with her huge, tragic ebony eyes and that husky voice that was tearing at their heartstrings. "Rory's Song" was a narrative ballad, and they knew it had been written by Sheena Reardon herself, immediately after her brother's death. It had never been recorded, and the rareness of its appearance in her repertoire made its effect doubly potent.

Sheena took a deep breath, her fingers stroking the strings of her guitar automatically. The first poignant note, as charged with emotion as a lightning bolt, soared over the darkened theater.

As he lay dying, my Rory asked me why.
I could find no answer, though God knows I tried."

She would only sing the words, Sheena thought

desperately. She would not think. She would not remember. But of course she did, and at last she allowed the memories to flow over her in an agonizing tide as they always did.

She was in a state of numbed shock for weeks after Rory's funeral, and she'd written "Rory's Song" only as an emotional outlet for her bewilderment and pain. She had written a few songs before and enjoyed singing them in her uncle's coffeehouse in Ballycraigh. When she first had sung "Rory's Song," it had been as a catharsis to release her pain in a desperate protest against the blow that had struck Rory down. It had not given her the release she craved, but she found that it had an incredible effect on her audience at the small coffeehouse. She was immediately approached to perform in concert and to her surprise, her uncle had given his wholehearted permission.

"It's only right that they remember what a good, brave lad your brother was, Sheena," he said with vigorous certainty. "While you sing 'Rory's Song,' they'll never be able to forget."

Under her uncle's direction, her career as a folksinger had taken off at a meteoric pace, and it wasn't long before he was forced to sell his coffeehouse and devote himself full time to his duties as her manager.

At first she received a certain amount of relief out of singing "Rory's Song." But as time passed and caused a healing scab to form on her initial pain, she found that singing the ballad opened the wound anew each time she sang it. She was always left as shaken and pain-racked as the morning Rory died.

This night was no exception. As the last, husky, pain-filled notes left her throat, there were silent tears running freely down her cheeks, and her dark eyes were as desolate and lost as those of a small child crying out in the night. She sat unmoving on her stool as the silence was broken by the sudden storm of applause that rolled in waves from the audience.

She felt numb with agony as she slowly rose to her feet and walked off the stage like an old, old woman.

Donal O'Shea was waiting in the wings, and she headed blindly for him like a sleepwalker. But suddenly he wasn't there before her any longer. O'Shea's square, sturdy figure was pushed roughly aside, and she was enfolded in strong, steely arms that cradled her with fierce possessiveness. Her head was pushed into a powerful, muscular chest, and she was hazily aware of a familiar heady scent. Challon, she thought confusedly, as she clung to the blessed security of his rock-hard body. What was he doing here?

Evidently several other people were wondering the same thing, for she heard a babble of outraged voices over the strong, muffled beat of Challon's heart. He apparently was paying little attention to their protests, for his arms didn't slacken, and his hand on her hair began to stroke her with the tenderness of a mother soothing a hurt child.

It must have been a full two minutes before he pushed her gently away, his amber gaze searching her face keenly. "Okay?" he murmured.

She nodded hesitantly, curiously unwilling to give up that blissful feeling of security, which was the greatest she had ever known.

"Good," he said briskly, and instead of releasing her, he pulled her into the curve of his arm as he turned to face a bristling Donal O'Shea and an equally annoyed Sean Reilly.

O'Shea stepped forward belligerently and placed a proprietary hand on Sheena's arm. "Come along, lass," he said, frowning. "You're so upset you don't know what you're about."

"Don't touch her, O'Shea." Challon's voice was as deadly as a laser ray. Sheena looked up in startled amazement at the change that had taken place in Challon. The amber gold eyes were no longer concerned and gentle but lit with the predatory hunger of a jungle animal as they glared at her uncle. "You let her go out there and tear herself to pieces!" he said fiercely. "I'm tempted to break every bone in your body very, very slowly."

O'Shea's face reddened with anger, and he muttered a curse beneath his breath. He growled, "Let's see you try it, me lad."

Reilly stepped forward, and there was a warning note in his voice as he said hastily, "Donal, I don't believe you've met Mr. Challon. Rand Challon?"

"I don't care who the hell he is!" O'Shea shouted. "He can't talk—" He broke off, and his eyes narrowed thoughtfully. "Rand Challon?"

"None other," Challon said coldly. "But don't let that stop you, O'Shea."

Sheena could see her uncle mentally grappling for control, and to some degree he succeeded. He forced himself to smile ingratiatingly. "I'm afraid there's a bit of a misunderstanding here, Mr. Challon. You seem to think my niece is some kind of victim. She'll tell you herself that she understands the necessity of certain unpleasant nuances of her work and that she's perfectly willing."

"She's willing because you've brainwashed her until she's nothing but a mindless pawn, O'Shea," Challon said in a grim tone. "It made me sick to my stomach to see her out there tonight. I'll be damned if I'll let you manipulate her any longer!"

"You'll forgive me if I fail to see how my niece's career is any of your concern, Mr. Challon," O'Shea said. "I believe that my assistant mentioned that you'd just met Sheena last evening. I'd be foolish to offend such an important person as yourself, but I must insist that you refrain from interfering."

"The hell I will." Challon's arm tightened about Sheena's slim waist. "She's never going to go through what she did tonight ever again."

O'Shea's eyes narrowed, and his lips tightened. "You have a rather notorious reputation with women, Mr. Challon, but surely even you can see that Sheena isn't the type of companion you're accustomed to. Why don't you leave the lass alone? Sheena is quite content with her life. She doesn't want or need your assistance."

"Why don't you ask her?" Challon asked arrogantly. "I realize that it's not your custom, but it is her life!"

"Why not?" O'Shea turned to Sheena and smiled lovingly. "Sheena?" He held out his hand in silent invitation.

Sheena shook her head dazedly. They were demanding that she choose between them, but surely there was only one choice she could make? What did she know of Challon other than the fact that he possessed a physical attraction that was well nigh irresistible? She didn't even know why he had been following her or what he really wanted of her.

She made a motion to free herself from Challon's iron hold, and she heard her uncle give a low, triumphant laugh.

Challon swore and turned her so that he could look down into her face. His fierce scowl gradually faded as he read the confused, unhappy expression on her thin, tear-streaked face.

"Poor little dove," he said gently. "It's all come too soon, hasn't it?" He released her reluctantly. "Fly away, little bird, but it's for the last time."

Her uncle grasped her arm firmly as Sheena moved slowly away from Challon. "Now that the matter is resolved, perhaps you'd better leave, Mr. Challon," he said briskly. "Sheena has had enough of an upset for one evening."

Challon nodded absently, his pensive gaze on Sheena's face. "Yes, I'll leave. You've won this round, O'Shea." His amber eyes lit with a burning ferocity. "But it's the last one I'll let you take."

"We'll have to see about that, won't we, Mr. Challon?" O'Shea said genially. His possessive arm drew Sheena closer.

Challon's narrowed eyes noted the gesture before shrugging casually and turning away. "Enjoy your victory," he said coolly. He turned back suddenly and spoke to Sheena. "I'm afraid this puts an end to my good intentions, sweetheart. I'm not the most patient man in the world at my best, and I'm mad as hell at the moment. It's only fair to warn you that from now on the gloves are off."

She frowned in bewilderment. "I don't know what you're talking about."

His smile was filled with loving sweetness. "I know you don't, little dove. But you will soon." He turned and strode down the hallway toward the stage door.

Sheena drew a deep breath of relief as she shut the door of the dressing room behind her and leaned on it for a brief instant. This final concert in New York had been as enthusiastically received as all the others, but she was glad it was over. Now the only items on her schedule in the next few weeks before the benefit were a number of personal appearances. Perhaps she'd finally get that rest that her uncle had been promising her.

But first there was O'Daniels's party to get through. Her uncle had been very insistent that she attend, so she thought, she'd better shower and be on her way. She stripped off her black silk dress and underthings and stuffed her hair into a shower cap. As she stepped into the small shower cubicle adjoining the dressing room, she wondered if she dared return to the hotel and call her uncle at O'Daniels's penthouse and plead weariness.

She shook her head resignedly as she realized the effect of this action. This was the first time since Challon's appearance at the concert five days earlier that she hadn't had either a solicitous Sean Reilly or Uncle Donal himself at her side constantly. She'd been practically smothered by their loving attention. The only reason she'd been allowed to make her own way to the party tonight was that her uncle and Sean were in a meeting O'Daniels had called just before the party.

She turned off the water reluctantly after a quick shower and drifted off hurriedly. Her uncle had hung the gown he wished her to wear on the door, and she reached for it with a vague feeling of displeasure. It was not black like her stage costume but a soft Quaker gray. She did get so tired of these eternal grays, blacks, and whites. Just once she would like to take on the brilliant plumage of a cardinal or a bluebird, she thought as she dressed.

She felt an odd twinge of pain as she remembered Challon's remark about transforming her from a dove to a lark. She hadn't seen Rand Challon since that night, despite that last cryptic warning he had uttered. She should be grateful of the fact, she assured herself staunchly. His presence had caused her nothing but problems.

Uncle Donal and Sean had been extremely wary and watchful after Challon's foreboding exit, she reflected. For the first time since Rory's death, her uncle had been positively sharp with her; he had insisted on her not seeing Challon again.

Challon had appeared on her horizon like a bolt of lightning and disappeared just as quickly. Perhaps it had amused the great man to challenge and bewilder the little Irish entertainer, she thought with an odd hurt. Well, evidently he had lost interest in his game, and she was well rid of him. Her life was once again on an even keel, and she could devote herself to her career with no disturbing, golden-eyed playboy to upset her.

She quickly brushed her dark tangle of curls and added a touch of makeup before pulling her black velvet cloak carelessly about her shoulders. She cast one last glance at the somber woman in the mirror, then flipped the light switch and closed the door.

The theater was deserted now, and her footsteps echoed hollowly on the wooden floor as she walked quickly to the stage door. The attendant on duty was a young, sandy-haired man in his early twenties, who looked up with a friendly grin as she approached.

"Your taxi is waiting outside in the alley, Miss Reardon," he said. "Mr. O'Shea asked me to arrange for it the minute you came offstage."

Sheena smiled gravely. "Thank you. That was very considerate of you."

"My pleasure," he said breezily, as he opened the stage door for her. "Let me help you down those steps. The outside light is burned out, and I haven't gotten around to changing it."

Sheena was grateful for the firm hand beneath her elbow as she negotiated the short flight of steps. The alley was almost pitch dark with only the headlights of an occasional passing car from the traffic on the far cross street. There was a yellow cab waiting only a few yards from the stage door with a shadowy driver barely discernible behind the wheel.

"I'll be fine now," Sheena told her escort as they stopped before the rear door of the taxi. "Thank you for your help."

The young man opened the car door. "Good night, Miss Reardon, have a pleasant evening." His hand beneath her elbow suddenly propelled her forward so strongly that she almost fell into the backseat of the taxi.

"Damn it, not so rough! You know what he said he'd do to us if we hurt her!" The masculine voice was harsh, but the grasp of the man occupying the backseat of the taxi was gentle as he pulled her the rest of the way into the taxi.

Sheena's heart seemed to freeze in her breast as she struggled instinctively to free herself.

"Quiet down now," her shadowy captor said soothingly. "No one's going to hurt you."

"Let me go!" she gasped, as she wriggled frantically to avoid the large masculine form holding her immobile. "You can't do this!"

"Want to bet, honey?" came the breezy voice of the stage door attendant as he jumped into the taxi. "Get going, Peter," he ordered the driver.

The taxi took off with a screech of tires. Sheena's resistance increased as stark terror gave her additional strength. This couldn't be happening, she thought frantically. Kidnapping happened to other people, not to her. It was not as if she were a fabulously wealthy superstar. What could they hope to gain by this terrifying crime? Her breath was coming in little gasps as she twisted and kicked out at her captor.

"Damn it, pass me the towel," he growled. "We'll have to use it. I can't hold her without bruising her. She's putting up too much of a fight."

"If you're willing to accept the responsiblity. I'm not going to put my head on the block," the sandy-haired man said tersely, as he put the folded cloth into his cohort's hands.

"Thanks a lot," her captor said caustically. "Hold her for a minute." As the transfer was made, he put his hand under Sheena's chin and said, "Sorry, lady. I tried to make it easy on you."

Sheena opened her mouth to scream as her nose and mouth were covered by the towel. Were they going to suffocate her? The towel smelled sickeningly sweet, and she couldn't seem to get her breath as the cloth was pressed down more firmly. Then she knew nothing but the whirling darkness.

Three

The unremitting droning sound was a constant irritant to the nagging ache in her temples, and Sheena gave a little whimper of distress as she buried her face in the pillow to try to escape the noise.

"Easy, little dove, everything is going to be fine. You're safe now." The deep, masculine voice was almost crooning, and she felt vaguely comforted as she slowly opened her heavy lids.

Rand Challon was bending over her, a worried frown creasing his forehead, his golden eyes intent on her face. For some reason the sight of that hard, ruthless face filled her with an odd serenity despite the woozy disorientation she was experiencing.

"How are you?" Challon asked quietly, his hand tenderly pushing a silky curl away from her forehead.

"I'm sick," she answered solemnly, turning her cheek to rub it against his hand. He was so warm and strong, she thought hazily. Just touching his hard, firm flesh seemed to ease the shakiness and fear she felt. Fear? Why should she be afraid? she wondered dizzily.

"I know you are," Challon said grimly. "Damn it, I told them not to use chloroform. I damn near killed the idiots when they carried you on board the plane. You'll be all right in a few minutes. They didn't use enough to put you out for very long."

Chloroform? What was he talking about? What plane had she been carried aboard? "I don't understand," she muttered. As she looked dazedly at her surroundings, she felt a growing sense of panic. She *was* on a plane—and a very luxurious one at that. She was lying on a sumptuous cream velvet couch, and the other pieces in the room were done in shades of cream and gold that contrasted beautifully with the richness of the walnut paneling. The cabin was lit by one lamp on the table at the end of the couch, and the resulting dimness created a tranquil intimacy. There was a mirrored bar in the rear of the plane, and the effect was more of a luxurious lounge than the interior of a jet.

"Where am I?" she whispered, levering herself up to a sitting position. She flinched as the movement sent a rush of pain to her head. She really did feel dreadful.

"At the moment we're about two hundred miles north of Montreal, Canada," he said casually, as he stood up and moved leisurely toward the mirrored bar at the rear of the cabin. "Sit still. I'll get you a cup of coffee and something to settle your stomach."

She only heard the first sentence. Her eyes widened with shock. "Canada!" Her hand went to her hair distractedly as she tried to pierce the haze that was clouding her thinking process. Then she sat bolt upright. "You kidnapped me!" she accused incredulously.

"Right," Challon replied tersely, as he strolled back to her and handed her two white pills and a cup of black coffee. "These ought to make you feel a bit better."

"What are they?" she asked suspiciously, staring down at the pills.

"Nothing very lethal," Challon answered lightly. "Though I can't blame you for being cautious. I told you that the chloroform was a mistake that won't be repeated. I want you very alert and wide awake, little dove."

Sheena swallowed the pills and washed them down with a sip of coffee. "Stop calling me that," she said tersely. She leaned back against the arm of the couch and eyed him with disfavor. He was dressed in faded jeans that hugged the strong line of his thighs with loving detail and a red flannel shirt with sleeves rolled up to the elbow to reveal the powerful muscles of his forearms. The casual outfit suited him much better than the cosmopolitan suits he had worn before, but gave him an aura of electric, virile earthiness that she did not want to acknowledge at this moment.

"Would it be too much to ask why you've carried your little practical joke to these outlandish lengths, Mr. Challon?" Her nausea was beginning to subside, and she found that anger was replacing it.

"It's no joke," he said, as he sat down on the couch and leaned back lazily. "I realized that I wasn't going to be able to pry you away from O'Shea and Reilly by more civilized means. They had much too strong a hold on you. I decided that I couldn't wait any longer to act after the concert that night." His face darkened with the memory. "So I arranged to 'liberate' you."

"Liberate!" she sputtered, her dark eyes flashing indignantly. "You kidnapped me! Well, you can't get away with it. Uncle Donal will have the police on your trail by now. Kidnapping is a very serious crime, you know."

"I love that little brogue you develop when you get excited," he said. Then he grinned and stretched his jean-clad legs before him. "I'm sorry to disillusion you, love, but I *can* get away with it. I could spirit you away and keep you indefinitely if I wished. It just takes a bit of manipulating for a man in my position. I admit that since you're in the public spotlight, it would be more expensive, but it could definitely be done."

Then as he noted the sudden panic in her face, he quickly dropped the ruthless objectivity in his manner and moved closer to enfold her in his arms. "Hey, it's going to be all right," he murmured. "I didn't mean to frighten you. I just have to make you see that it's useless to put up a fight. I had notes very expertly forged and sent to both your uncle and James O'Daniels explaining that you were exhausted and were going away for a bit of a rest. They'll receive notes periodically in the coming months assuring them of your continued good health."

"Months!" Sheena said, startled. She pushed away from him and looked into his face. "You can't mean to keep me that long. That's carrying your little joke too far."

He shook his head. "I intend to keep you forever," he said. "But I figured it might take a few months for you to come around to my way of thinking on the subject."

She was astounded. "You're certifiably insane," she pronounced with utmost surety.

He nodded. "That's entirely possible. I realized some time ago that I was completely obsessed where you're concerned."

"But why?" she whispered, bewildered. "You don't even know me. Why should you go to such outrageous lengths just because you have some absurd idea that I need to be rescued?"

He touched the hollow of her cheek with a gentle finger. "I'm not that quixotic, love. My reasons for taking you were entirely selfish. After the party that night, I couldn't sleep for thinking about you. Then when I saw what O'Shea did to you the next night at the concert, I decided that I wasn't going to wait any longer to have you belong to me."

"Why me?" she demanded in exasperaton, a scowl darkening her face. "Uncle Donal says you have no problem acquiring women. Why don't you go kidnap one of them and let me go? You know very well you're only doing this because I represent some sort of challenge. You couldn't possibly have developed a deathless passion for me. We don't even belong to the same world!"

"I can't argue that you represent a challenge," he said, grinning, his lion eyes dancing. "You may prove to be the most difficult one I've ever encountered, but I'm not the type you seem to think. My desire is to drag you into bed and ravish that lovely nubile body, but I'm trying to restrain my baser instincts until you get to know me a little better."

"You wouldn't," Sheena whispered, her eyes widening apprehensively.

"I would," Challon assured her firmly. "But only as a last resort. I'm fairly certain that once you're my mistress, you won't want to leave me. But I don't want a confused little girl in my bed. I want a full-blooded woman who will demand as much from me as I will from her." He sighed ruefully. "I sure hope you're a fast learner, dove. I'm definitely not used to celibacy."

"And how do you expect to perform this transformation?" she asked tartly. "It surely won't be easy to reform such a colorless specimen as you think me." She slapped his hand away from her face sharply.

Challon chuckled. "You're already changing," he drawled, his golden eyes twinkling. "I knew that all I'd have to do was remove you from O'Shea's influence and your natural personality would emerge. Now all I have to do is to sit back and wait until you're ripe for the plucking."

The arrogance of the man! Did he really think she'd stand for this sort of treatment? Her black eyes were blazing as she drew back as far from him as the couch permitted. "You won't have the opportunity," she said angrily. "As soon as we get off this plane, I'm leaving. Unless you keep me chained or locked up, I'll find a way to get away from you. And when I do, I'll see that you're thrown into jail like any other criminal!"

He seemed more pleased than upset by this defiance. "That's it, love, come alive," he encouraged her softly, his eyes on her flushed face. "Anger and hate are not the emotions I'm looking for, but at least they're a beginning."

"You're impossible!" Sheena cried. "Don't you understand? I won't stay with you!"

"In about fifteen minutes we'll be landing at our destination. I have a cabin in the woods that's about a hundred miles from the nearest inhabited town. I don't think I have to tell you that trying a trek like that in Canada in November would be the equivalent of suicide."

"What about the pilot?" she asked belligerently. "Perhaps he won't be so willing to take on the role of criminal accomplice."

"All my employees are completely loyal to me," Challon said. "They're paid exorbitantly well to be. Besides, the question is immaterial. After John drops us off, he'll return to Montreal and wait there until I radio him to come and get us."

"You think you have it all arranged. Well, I'd rather freeze to death than stay cooped up with an arrogant, chauvinistic egomanic who thinks he runs the world!"

"You'll change your mind," Challon assured her. "Once you cool down, you'll realize how futile running away would be."

Suddenly Sheena felt as if she were going up in flames of rage and frustration. She wasn't even conscious that her arm was moving until her hand connected with a sharp crack on Challon's cheek. She gave a shocked gasp as she saw the red imprint of her fingers appear on his lean, tanned cheek. Her hand went to her mouth, and she unconsciously shrank farther away from him. "I didn't mean to do that," she said faintly.

Challon's golden eyes were blazing for a brief instant, and she felt a moment of sheer panic. Then the anger was gone, and his face turned somber. "That was a mistake," he said quietly. "I've been sitting here for two hours watching you sleep and wishing that pillow you were cuddling up to was me. I almost took you in my arms a hundred times, but somehow I held on to my control. Then you use the surest method known to man to break it." His hands reached out and closed on her arms and drew her inexorably into his embrace. "I think you owe me, little dove."

"No!" she cried desperately, shaking her head and straining away from him. "Please, don't do this."

"I have to," he said huskily. "Don't be afraid. I'm not going to take more than you want to give. I just have to touch you. I've been in a fever for you for so long. I have to have a little something or go crazy."

"But I . . ." The rest of Sheena's protest was lost as Challon's warm mouth covered hers. His lips were hot and smooth as he coaxed her with devastating expertise to respond. She found the embrace held a dizzying excitement as his lips moved with a ravaging tenderness to the curve of her cheek and then to the lobe of her ear.

"Your bones are so delicate," he murmured, as he nibbled at her ear. "I feel as if I could break you with one hand." His tongue plunged hotly in her ear, and she shuddered helplessly as a melting languor flooded her and she sagged weakly against his warm strength. Challon fell back on the couch, bringing her with him so that she was lying on top of him, the weight of her body pressing her breathlessly close to his hard, taut muscles.

He rolled over so that they were facing each other on the narrow couch, and his hand touched the gray crepe of the gown at the breast. "I hate you in this," he muttered, as his lips searched out the throbbing pulse in the hollow of her throat. "I want you always to be surrounded with brilliance and joy." His tongue was probing the hollow with a provocativeness that caused her breath to catch in her throat. "I want to see you in scarlet satin and yellow chiffon." His lips moved up to cover hers in a long, hot kiss, his tongue exploring her teeth and tongue with ravishing thoroughness. "But most of all I want to see you in nothing at all!"

His hands slid the grey crepe from her shoulders, and with a multitude of lazy kisses, he began an intimate exploration of her shoulders. His hands were now running curiously over her slim back and hips. He buried his face in her hair to murmur huskily, "You're so small and slender. Do you know how many times I've imagined how tight you'd feel around me?" Then at her shocked gasp, he chuckled deep in his chest. "Sorry, love, I know that I'm going too fast for you." He gave her one last lingering kiss before he reluctantly sat up. He looked down at her flushed face and languid dark eyes and gave a deep sigh. "You'd better sit up and get away from me, little dove. You were pretty damn close to joining the mile-high club just now."

She looked up at him, still dazed from his passionate lovemaking. "What's that?" she asked, her gaze fixed on the beautifully sensual curve of his lips.

He chuckled again, his golden eyes twinkling. "Never mind. I keep forgetting that convent upbringing." He rose lightly to his feet and strode to the bar and poured himself a whiskey from a crystal decanter. "I'll demonstrate some other time—in detail." He grinned. "Graphic detail." He poured a small amount of whiskey in another glass and strolled back to her. "You'd better drink this," he said, his lips still twitching. "You're a little shaky. Which makes me pleased as punch, I might add." He watched her tenderly as she sat up and hurriedly arranged the bodice of her dress before reaching for the glass. "When Reilly appeared on the scene, I was afraid he was brought in to be prince consort, but you're still green as grass, little dove. All that passion is just waiting there for me to tap it. God, I'm glad!"

Sheena took a few experimental sips of the whiskey and then handed the glass back to him. The liquor caused a surge of heat in her blood that did serve to steady her, but it also cleared her head of the sensual euphoria that Challon had generated with his sexual magnetism. Shamed color flooded her cheeks. Good God in heaven, what had she done! She'd allowed Challon to manipulate her body and emotions as if she were one of his eager harem of women. It was true that her career had allowed her no time to gain the experience he'd mentioned, but even a green girl should have known better than to allow herself to be swayed by Challon's powerful virility to such an extent. The man had disrupted the peacefully smooth tempo of her life. He had insulted her uncle. He had actually kidnapped her! Yet she had still allowed him to make love to her.

"I must have been mad," she muttered. Well, she was no longer under that mesmerizing spell. She squared her chin firmly and looked at him with defiance breathing out of every pore. "There's nothing waiting for you but a jail cell," she spat out. "I'll not be so easy for you to get around a second time, Mr. Challon. It was merely that I was sick and half out of my mind from that chloroform that made me so accommodating."

"Maybe I shouldn't have been so rough on the men who snatched you," Challon drawled, his lips twitching in amusement. "Though I've never heard that chloroform had aphrodisiac properties, and you certainly appear to be fully recovered."

A light suddenly went on over the door to the cockpit, and Challon glanced up swiftly. "Time to buckle up, sweetheart. We're starting our descent."

The "cabin" was certainly not the small, primitive log shack of her imaginings, Sheena thought sourly, as she waited shivering on the redwood porch while Challon unlocked the door. It was more like a luxurious country home.

As they had swiftly made their way up to the A-frame redwood cottage from the landing strip at the bottom of the hill, the moonlight had revealed the clean, modern lines of the charming cabin and the spacious redwood sundeck, which completely surrounded the house.

Challon flipped on the light and swiftly adjusted the thermostat beside the switch as he ushered her in the door. "Three bedrooms upstairs," he said briefly. "There's a kitchen/dining room down the hall to the left and a library adjoining the living room. Get used to it, little dove. It's going to be your home for quite a while."

Sheena shot him a lethal glance, which he cheerfully ignored as he moved swiftly to the massive stone fireplace on the far wall and knelt to light the wood that was stacked and ready.

"You certainly like to rough it, don't you?" Sheena asked caustically. Her gaze flicked around the spacious living room with its gleaming oak floors covered with Indian area rugs striped boldly in scarlet and cream. The long beige couch with its scarlet throw pillows in front of the fireplace was expertly crafted for quiet beauty and supreme comfort, as were the other pieces of furniture in the room.

Challon looked up and grinned as the fire caught and started to blaze cheerfully. "I figured that you're going to have enough adjustments to make without having to cope with life in the raw. If you want to sample a more simple life-style, I have a tiny cabin on an island in the Caribbean that you might enjoy. We'll go there in March, if you like."

Sheena's fists knotted, and she mentally counted to ten. Challon's casual assumption of their future together was positively maddening. "I don't want to go anywhere with you but back to New York," she said between clenched teeth. "Why can't you see that you just can't do this to me?"

"You'd better come closer to the fire," he said. He stood up and took off his sheepskin coat and threw it on the couch. "The temperature is dropping rapidly, and they're expecting snow tonight. I've turned up the thermostat, but it will take a while for it to get really warm in here."

He was ignoring her protests as if she had never uttered them, she noticed angrily. "I'm quite comfortable here," she said haughtily, pulling her cloak closer about her.

A flicker of golden fire lit Challon's eyes. "If you don't get over here, I'm coming to get you." His tone was softly menacing. "And we've already seen how any physical confrontation between us ends, haven't we?"

Sheena felt the embarrassed color rise to her cheeks, and she bit her lower lip uncertainly, debating whether she should defy him.

"Sheena!" The word had the crack of a whiplash, and she found herself hurriedly moving forward.

The blaze of the fire was undoubtedly comforting, but the gleam of satisfaction in Challon's eyes ruined any pleasure she might have felt in the additional warmth. "You needn't think that I'll let you order me about," she said crossly. "I just decided that I was a bit chilly after all."

"I see," Challon said gravely, that maddening twinkle back in his eyes. "How fortunate for me that you changed your mind."

She threw him a dark scowl and pointedly turned her back on him, stretching her hands out to the fire.

There was still a thread of amusement in his voice as he said, "Stay here and keep warm, and I'll see if I can rustle us up something to eat. The kitchen should be well stocked, I had a man fly out a few days ago with supplies."

"You needn't bother," Sheena said coolly. "I'm not hungry."

There was an obvious impatience in Challon's tone. "You've got to be hungry. I happen to know that you never eat before a performance. That probably means that you haven't had a bite since lunch yesterday, and it's now almost four in the morning."

Was there nothing that the man didn't know about her? Well, it would give her great pleasure to see that the arrogant Mr. Challon failed in this aim, at least. She turned to face him. "Nevertheless, I'm not hungry," she said firmly, receiving distinct satisfaction from the scowl that clouded his face.

"I don't give a damn if you're hungry or not," he growled, his frowning gaze running over her slim, fragile figure. "You're going to eat anyway. A strong wind would blow you away, and I won't have you getting sick."

"I'm sure that would be very awkward for you," Sheena bit out. "Then you might have a murder charge against you as well as one for kidnapping. Well, to hell with you, Rand Challon! You can't force me to eat."

Challon's lion eyes were blazing with a matching anger. "You stubborn little idiot. You'd probably starve yourself to death just to get a little of your own back against me. Do you envy your brother his foolish martyr's death so much that you want to imitate him?"

Sheena backed away, her eyes stricken. She felt as if he had physically struck her, so cruel was that last verbal blow.

There was a flicker of remorse in Challon's face as he took an impulsive step toward her. "Sheena—" he started gently.

"No!" she cried. "No!"

Then she was running blindly toward the front door. She heard him call her name stridently as she tore out on the redwood sundeck and down the stairs. She didn't even feel the frigid cold now, though she was vaguely conscious of the sharp wind hitting her tear-streaked face. In that moment she was almost totally mindless, her only motivation that of an animal in pain looking for a dark place to hide. She was scarcely aware of the sobs that were shaking her. She flew down the hill past the landing strip into the forest beyond.

She could hear Challon's voice roaring her name as he crashed through the bushes behind her, but she continued streaking through the forest like a frightened gazelle pursued by a lion.

Suddenly she stepped off the edge of the world and was falling into space! Then she was enveloped in water so cold that it robbed her of all body heat and precious breath. Her velvet cloak was immediately drenched, and the weight pulled her helplessly beneath the deadly surface.

She struggled desperately to fight her way back to the surface, but her sodden clothing was like a rock holding her down. She knew an instant of blinding panic as she realized incredulously that she was drowning. She was going to die. Perhaps she was already dying, for suddenly there was nothing but the icy darkness.

If the darkness had remained, it would have been bearable, but there were suddenly brilliant colors that shifted like a kaleidoscope, the hues melting and running into each other until they finally turned into that stark, sterile white that she recognized with a chilling horror. Hospital white.

"No, please!" she moaned, knowing what was to follow. For all the nightmares started like that. Then it was not a dream at all but reality once again.

It had been raining that day five years ago, that light misting Irish rain that her uncle always referred to as angels' tears. She'd been seventeen then and still at Saint Mary's Convent outside Ballycraigh. It was a very good school and the nuns exceptionally protective of their charges. Perhaps if they'd been less zealous in that respect, everything would have been different, she had thought later.

As it was, she'd heard nothing until her uncle had appeared at the mother superior's office to take her to the hospital in Ballycraigh. She'd been dazed and disbelieving as she'd stared blindly out the car window at the spring rain that was bringing vibrant new life to the green, rolling fields they were passing. Life. But it was not life she was going to, but death. Rory was dying in that white, sterile bed in Ballycraigh Hospital.

The tears were running down her face in a steady

stream now. "Why, Uncle Donal?" she asked bitterly. "Why would he do it? Why would they let him do it? He's only eighteen and has everything to live for."

Her uncle's hand reached over to enfold her own in a warm, comforting clasp. "I don't know, lass," he said huskily, his own gray eyes suspiciously bright. "I didn't even know he'd gotten politically involved at the university until I heard that they'd barricaded themselves in a classroom and were on a hunger strike. It was all so foolish," he continued brokenly. "Only the very young would think that in forty-five days they could change conditions that have existed for eight hundred years."

"But you said that the rest of the students gave up after only three weeks," Sheena said desperately. "Why didn't Rory?"

O'Shea shrugged helplessly. "You know how stubborn the lad can be when he sets his mind to something. He wouldn't give up. And by the time they broke in, it was too late. He'd developed pneumonia and was burning up with fever."

"But he can't be dying," she said sobbing. "Not Rory." Rory was the most joyously alive person she'd ever known. There was scarcely a moment when his dark eyes were not dancing with mischievous laughter or his lips curving in a smile from the sheer joy of living. "Why didn't someone tell me?"

Uncle Donal's voice was grave. "I tried to keep you out of it, lass. The reporters are making a circus of the whole tragic mess. Believe me, if Rory had a chance, I'd never have brought you into it, even now. But it's only fitting that you should say goodbye to your brother."

"You had no right to keep it from me," she charged fiercely. "I could have talked to him. He would have listened to me."

O'Shea shook his head sadly. "Do you think that I didn't try to persuade him to give it up? He just wouldn't listen. He's changed from the Rory you knew. You've only seen him on holidays for the last year."

"He hasn't changed," she denied fiercely. "You know how close we are. He'd have listened to me!"

"Perhaps you're right," he said wearily. "I did what I thought was best."

She cast a glance at his miserable face and felt a twinge of shame. Of course he had done what he thought was best. He had never done anything else since he'd taken her and Rory into his home six years before. "I know you did," she whispered, squeezing his hand. "I know."

When they drew up before the hospital, Sheena was given evidence of the media circus that her uncle had mentioned. The two of them were instantaneously pounced on at the curbside by reporters and cameramen. She flinched involuntarily as a barrage of flashbulbs went off in her face as her uncle quickly ushered her into the sanctuary of the hospital.

Rory didn't die until early the following morning, and she sat with him all through that long, agonizing night watching him struggle for breath behind the icily impersonal oxygen tent.

He only roused enough to speak to her once, and then she had to lean close to make out the words.

"Sheena."

Her hand tightened on his skeletally thin one. "Yes, love, I'm here."

His dark eyes so like her own were searching. "Proud of me?" he croaked, just a hint of his old boyish smile on his emaciated face.

She could feel the tears flood her eyes. She wanted to cry and beat her fists on his chest in frustration, to shout and rage at him that there was no cause that was worth his life. But she knew she couldn't deprive him of the only gift that might give his sacrifice meaning.

"Yes, I'm very proud of you, love," she said huskily, her throat aching with tears.

He sighed contentedly. "Glad. Uncle Donal's proud of me, too." His lids closed, and for a moment she thought he'd fainted. Then his eyes flicked open, and there was a trace of panic in their depths. "I don't want to die, Sheena," he whispered desperately, bruising her hand in a sudden surge of strength. "Why?"

She was never to know what he meant by that last desperate cry, for Rory had lapsed once again into unconsciousness and died a little over an hour later.

It was two days before Sheena realized that she, too, hadn't died but had entered a torturous inferno of feverish pain and nightmarish dreams.

During that time, she was sent rocketing into an almost hysterical dependence on the only solid figure in a constantly shifting universe. The man with the tawny sun-streaked hair and gentle golden eyes was always there when she threw off the heavy covers or cried out for water. When she woke in the night screaming as she relived over and over that nightmare in the hospital in Ballycraigh, it was the golden man who enfolded her in strong, comforting arms and wiped her streaming eyes, his expression frighteningly grim despite the tenderness of his touch.

And when her body was racked with chills and no amount of blankets could alleviate the icy cold that seemed to pervade her bones, it was the golden man who lay holding her in his arms, his warm body giving her its blessed heat, while his hands caressed and soothed her aching muscles and his voice crooned an affectionate litany in her ear.

Even when she became well enough to realize that the golden man was Rand Challon, she still could not rid herself of that curious dependence that seemed as much emotional as physical. She was still enfolded in an exhausted lassitude that caused her to feel not the slightest embarrassment or discomfort as he performed the most intimate of services for her.

Nor did he seem to view his duties with anything but the most matter-of-fact naturalness. Ignoring the silence that she was too weary to break, he bathed her, brushed her hair, and fed her as if she were a much-loved child. While he was going about these functions, he kept up a cheerful, inconsequential chatter that demanded no answer from her. In its own way, this was as comforting as the way he lounged lazily in an easy chair by her bed when she slept so that his warm, quiet smile was the first thing she saw when she awoke.

It was almost a week after she'd arrived at the cabin before her weariness dissipated enough for her to ask the questions that had seemed oddly unimportant in the past several days. She had wakened from an afternoon nap to see Challon in his usual brown leather easy chair beside the bed. His golden eyes were fixed absently into space, and there was a frown creasing his forehead. For the first time Sheena noticed the lines of weariness about his mouth and the faint shadows beneath his eyes. He was dressed in beige cord pants and brown suede shirt, and Sheena's lips twitched unexpectedly. Lion colors for a golden man.

As if feeling her appraisal, his gaze swooped down and met hers. Immediately his frown vanished, and his bronzed face lit with an affectionate smile. "Back with us again?" he asked cheerfully, obviously not expecting an answer. "These naps are getting shorter all the time. Pretty soon you'll be able to do without them entirely." He stood up and stretched lazily, and Sheena was suddenly breathlessly aware of his lean, virile strength. "I'll just run downstairs and see what Laura's prepared for your supper."

He turned away only to whirl back to face her as she asked slowly, "Who's Laura?"

The smile that illuminated his face this time was as brilliant as the sun coming up. "Thank God," he said fervently, his body relaxing from the tension that he had kept carefully hidden from her. He sank back into the easy chair beside her bed and took her hand in both of his. "The doctor said that it would only be a matter of time," he continued. "But you were scaring the hell out of me, sweetheart."

"Who is Laura?" Sheena asked again, frowning. For some reason the idea of another woman intruding on this strange intimacy that existed between them filled her with distinct displeasure.

"You'll meet her presently," Challon replied, with most unsatisfactory vagueness. His keen eyes were swiftly raking her face, noting the alertness of her expression and the snapping darkness of her eyes, which had previously held only languid acceptance and disinterest. "How do you feel?"

Sheena considered the question solemnly. "Hungry," she said decisively.

The reply was met with a jubilant laugh from Challon. "Great!" Rising to his feet again, he headed for the door. "Laura was getting fed up fixing you that sick-room pap."

Laura again. Sheena bit her lower lip vexedly. Evidently Laura's opinion loomed large in Challon's scheme of things. She refused to ask herself why this disturbed her so, and firmly turned her attention to examining her surroundings. She must have been vaguely aware of the decor of the room during the past days, but it had never actually sunk beyond that exhausted lethargy.

The room was surprisingly spacious for a guest room and had a cozy cheerfulness due to the blazing, crackling fire in the fireplace across the room. Though only late afternoon, the room had a twilight dimness due to the drawn red plaid drapes that covered the windows that spanned one whole wall. The spread on the bed was also a red tartan plaid, as was the throw that was tossed carelessly on the beige chaise longue before the fireplace. The carpet was a plush creamy beige and contrasted beautifully with the polished cherrywood of the contemporary furnishings. There was a painting above the fireplace by Keane, and she studied the picture curiously. It was a portrait of a small child who possessed the enormous dark, sad eyes that were the artist's trademark. It was oddly out of place in a room that projected such vibrant cheerfulness, Sheena thought.

"Think you can work your way through a small steak?" Challon asked briskly, as he entered the room carrying a tray. "It's best not to overload your stomach at first."

Sheena nodded eagerly and levered herself hurriedly to a sitting position, only to clutch the sheet up to her chin with a shocked cry. She was totally nude!

"Oops, I forgot about that," Challon said, grinning mischievously as he put the tray on the bedside table. He strode quickly across the room, opened the top drawer in the cherrywood bureau, and drew out a filmy gown in a brilliant shade of sunshine yellow. Grabbing a matching bed jacket, he returned to the bed. He slipped the gown over her head and then lifted her to smooth the gown down around her with impersonal efficiency. He put her arms in the bed jacket before giving her a kiss on her surprised lips and turning away to retrieve the tray and place it on her lap. "I'm going to miss seeing you naked as Eve," he said, winking outrageously as the color flooded her cheeks.

"Was that really necessary?" she asked faintly, her eyes avoiding his as she carefully buttered a crusty warm roll.

He dropped back down in the brown leather easy chair and stretched his legs before him lazily. "Well, I told myself it was," he drawled, then grinned shamelessly. "It made things much easier nursing you. Besides, looking at you was the only enjoyable aspect of the entire hellish week. I figured that I deserved it."

Somehow this did not even raise a spark of indignation in Sheena. The intimacy that had evolved between them since her illness had inexplicably quenched her former antagonism. How could she object to him seeing her naked when she could vaguely remember crying out to be held in his arms through the long, frightening hours of the darkness? He had given to her with complete selflessness and dedication and had forged bonds that she would now find almost impossible to break.

"What happened to me?" she asked quietly, as she took a bite of the slightly rare steak. "I gather I've been quite ill?"

He nodded his head. "You fell into the lake," he said, his face turning grim at the memory. "I got you out before you drowned, but you were still suffering from hypothermia. That lake is glacier cold this time of year. I carried you back to the cabin and put you to bed and then radioed for the doctor." He raised a sandy eyebrow inquiringly. "Do you remember Dr. Knowleton?"

She shook her head, and he said, "I didn't think you would. You were pretty much out of your head by the time he arrived. You were alternating between chills and fever, and I was almost out of my mind." He leaned forward suddenly and closed his hand over her blanket-covered thigh. "Don't you ever do that to me again, do you hear?" he said hoarsely, his expression fierce. "I thought you were going to die before Knowleton got here."

Then as he met her wide, startled eyes, his hand loosened, and he sat back in the chair and relaxed. "Sorry, I didn't mean to frighten you. Go on with your dinner," he said, wearily running his hand through his tawny hair. "Knowleton said that you were not only suffering from shock but prolonged exhaustion and anemia." He scowled darkly, "Plus a slight case of malnutrition. Your loving uncle certainly took great care of you!" Then as she would have protested, he made an impatient wave with his hand. "Well, that's water under the bridge. He won't get another chance with you now. Even after you got over the shock, I couldn't rouse you from that damned lethargy. The doctor said it was just exhaustion and that you'd snap out of it yourself in time." He shook his head ruefully. "He didn't mention that I'd almost go nuts before you got around to it."

"You took very good care of me," she said gravely. "I was aware of that, at least." She hadn't noticed before that his eyes crinkled up at the corners when he smiled, she thought.

"I guess it goes with the territory. But you can bet I'll be a damn sight more careful the next time I kidnap a lovely lady. It can obviously be a very tricky proposition."

Her lips curved in a little smile, and her dark eyes twinkled with amusement. "You're planning on making a practice of it, then?"

Challon's expression took on an intentness that caused sudden warmth to flood her veins with a sweet langour. "No," he said thickly. "Once is enough, little dove."

He reached over and picked up the napkin on the tray and dabbed her lips gently. "Butter," he said huskily. "I was tempted to remove it in a considerably more erotic manner, but I have to keep reminding myself that you're still an invalid."

She shook her head resignedly, and a low chuckle of amusement broke from her. "You're utterly daft," she said, as she finished the last bite of steak and pushed the plate away.

There was a warm gentleness in her expression that brought a searching thoughtfulness to Challon's face. "You're not angry with me any more, are you?" he asked quietly.

She shook her head. "No, I'm not angry." She took a sip of tea. "It's very difficult holding on to a grudge against someone who's not only saved my life but has taken care of me in the way you have."

He frowned. "I don't want your gratitude. I only want you to promise not to do anything foolish like trying to run away from me again."

She shook her head slowly, her dark eyes grave. "I can't give you that promise. I have obligations to fulfill. My Uncle Donal and Sean will be very worried if I don't return soon." Holding the teacup, she leaned back against the pillows. "At first, I thought that your actions were those of a bored playboy looking for a new game to play, but I've changed my mind." She looked up to meet his eyes earnestly. "For some reason, you sincerely believe that I need rescuing. But can't you see how wrong you are? My uncle has never been anything but kindness itself to me, and I've never been forced to do anything that I didn't want to do. There are just some duties that must be performed even though there is a little pain involved."

"A little pain!" He snorted, his lips twisting bitterly. "Don't try to make light of it, damn it. Remember, I was the one who was holding you when those night-mares were ripping you apart. If I'd had your loving Uncle Donal here then, I'd have strangled him with my bare hands."

Then his expression lost its grimness as he saw her troubled face. He bent forward swiftly and kissed her lightly on the tip of her nose. "We won't argue about it now. I'd be foolish to push my luck when I've made so many gains already. You have my permission to make all the escape attempts you like as long as you don't put yourself in danger again. In return for my gracious leniency, would it be too much to ask that you just put aside your very solemn 'duties' and let me teach you how to play, little dove?" He smiled coaxingly, his golden eyes twinkling. "You might just as well give in to the big, bad kidnapper until you can wrest yourself from my clutches. No one can blame you for submitting to the inevitable."

"It depends on what you consider 'play,' " Sheena said cautiously, her spirits rising to meet the reckless challenge in Challon's face. It was true that she couldn't help her situation at the moment. Would it be so wrong to let Challon demonstrate what he'd meant when he said he would transform her into a lark?

He arched a brow. "If you expect a promise that I won't try to seduce you, you're not going to get it," he said frankly. "I fully intend to get you into my bed at the earliest opportunity. That's going to be number one on my list of priorities." One tender finger reached out to trace the passionate curve of her lips. "I guarantee that you're going to enjoy those particular lessons most of all. The only promise you'll get from me on that score is that you'll want it just as much as I do."

"You're very confident."

"You're damn right I am. You've already seen the kind of chemistry we have working for us. I believe that I'm experienced enough to know how to pleasure you, love." His lion eyes twinkled teasingly. "I wasn't brought up in a convent or had a dragon uncle protecting *my* virtue!"

That fact was more than evident, Sheena thought crossly. He'd probably had women standing in line to receive that mocking grin since he was in kindergarten. Well, he wouldn't find her so easy to manipulate, she thought. Challon was a charming and companionable man, and there was no real reason why she should not enjoy a brief holiday until she could convince him to release her. She obviously needed a rest, as was evidenced by the physical breakdown she had suffered. Challon was so sure of his powers of persuasion that she had no fear that he would use any form of coercion to force her to a sexual commitment. She had every confidence that she would be as safe as she wanted to be.

His golden eyes were narrowed like those of a pouncing cat. "What about it, little dove? Truce?"

For an instant she felt a moment of apprehension as she met that predatory gaze. Was she underestimating the power and determination of the man? There was little doubt that despite the curious tenderness that he displayed to her, he was a very dangerous man. Then she shrugged off the worrisome thought. She absolutely refused to let fanciful imaginings cause her to be intimidated.

"Truce," she agreed firmly, setting the cup back in its saucer. She was rewarded by a brilliant smile that was so tender that it caused a strange flutter somewhere near her heart.

"I'll see that you don't regret it," he said quietly, as he rose to his feet and picked up the tray from her lap. "I'll get rid of this tray and be back in a minute. I think you'd better stay in bed and rest for today." As he headed for the door, he glanced back over his shoulder to ask, "Do you play chess?"

"No," she answered. "I've never bothered to learn."

"I'll teach you." He grinned. "It's a great way to hone up your strategic skills. I've never enjoyed an easy victory."

Her lips curved in a reluctant smile as he opened the door. Then her smile faded, and a frown crossed her brow. "Rand!" she called impulsively. When he looked back inquiringly, she asked, "Who's Laura?"

He gave her a grin that held an element of mischief. "I think I'll let you wonder about that for a while. They say a little spice of jealousy can be a healthy ingredient to any relationship." He closed the door softly behind him.

Four

Sheena was not destined to meet Laura Bradford until the next morning.

Challon had given permission for Sheena to come downstairs for breakfast, and she realized that she was very eager to leave her sickbed behind her. She found that she was only a little shaky when she got out of bed and made her way to the adjoining bathroom to shower and wash her hair. Then, feeling considerably better, she returned to the bedroom to search out something to wear.

There was more than a generous selection in the built-in closet and the bureau drawers, she discovered. They contained everything from the most fragile underwear to designer jeans and imported bulky knit sweaters. She was amused to note that except for the jeans, everything was in hues that rivaled the peacock for brilliance. Evidently Challon had been quite sincere in his hatred for her drab, somber wardrobe and had supplied her with one to his own taste. It didn't even surprise her that everything was in her size. A man as thorough as Challon would hardly slip up on a minor detail such as that.

She pulled on a pair of designer jeans and a stunning scarlet and white ski sweater. She made a face as she noticed the slight looseness in the waist of the jeans. Well, the fit was almost perfect. Challon couldn't be expected to have anticipated the weight loss due to her illness. Her face was thinner, too, she noticed gloomily, as she brushed her dark gypsy curls into some sort of order.

In fact, the image that looked out of the mirror was so delicate and fragile-looking that she gave a sigh of discouragement. Even the stunning scarlet of the sweater could not turn her into the exciting, full-blooded woman that Challon had said was his ideal. His purported obsession for her would probably be a temporary aberration that would fade with lightning rapidity when he recognized that she had none of the sophisticated appeal of his usual female companions. It wouldn't surprise her if he jetted her back to her own world even faster than he'd whisked her away. She was careful not to ask herself why this thought caused her to feel a sudden moroseness. Slipping into brown dockside strollers, she left the bedroom.

Challon was waiting in the hallway at the foot of the stairs, and there was no hint of disappointment in his face as his gaze went over her with lingering thoroughness as she came down the stairs. When she reached the third step from the bottom, he grasped her slim waist in both his hands and swung her down the last steps. He gave her a quick, hard kiss before putting her down.

When she would have protested, he said softly, "I missed you. Do you know that last night was the first night since we arrived here that I haven't slept with you?" He chuckled as her eyes widened in shock. "Of course you probably don't remember much of it, but I found it very pleasant to have you curled up so trust-ingly in my arms."

He was wrong. She remembered quite vividly snug-gling up to the golden man on several occasions, but she hadn't realized that he had slept with her as a matter of course. She could feel the color flood her cheeks as she remembered that she apparently had been completely nude during that entire week.

He chuckled again as he noticed her sudden dis-composure. Keeping one arm around her waist, he turned her in the direction of the kitchen. "Come along and meet Laura," he said.

With its glowing maple cabinets and early American decor, the combination kitchen/dining room had a col-orful hominess. The polished maple dining table and red-gingham cushioned captain's chairs fronted an oval brick fireplace that contained a cheerful fire.

Challon propelled Sheena past the dining area to a tall, elegant figure standing with her back to them at the stove. Slipping his arms about the woman's waist, he planted a light kiss on the nape of her neck. "Sheena, this is my best girl, Laura Bradford."

The woman turned and leveled a stern eye at Challon. "If you don't stop your hell-raising and fooling around, I'll be the only girl who will have you, Rand Challon," she said tartly.

Laura Bradford was a woman in her middle sixties and undoubtedly one of the plainest women Sheena had ever met. The older woman was almost painfully thin and just a shade under six feet. Her short mousy brown hair was thin and permed into a riot of curls framing a freckled face whose only charm lay in a pair of exceptionally fine eyes, the color of rich brandy. Her unimpressive appearance, however, was more than off-set by the character in her face and the chic elegance of the navy blue slacks and heavy silk Dior smock that she wore.

"Laura, my love, you cut me to the quick," Challon said mournfully, his golden eyes dancing. "Now hold that razor tongue of yours and say good morning to Sheena." He turned to Sheena and explained. "Laura practically raised me from the time I was four. She was first my nanny and then my governess. When I realized that I might need help when you became ill, I sent out an SOS, and she left her teaching job in Houston and came running."

Sheena smiled shyly. "I'm sorry to be such a nuisance. Rand said you hated to cook sickroom meals."

Laura Bradford grimaced. "I hate to cook, period," she said. "I eat most of my meals out when I'm in Houston. But you were no trouble. In fact, I was glad for something to do. Rand wouldn't let anyone else near you." She shot him a cross look. "For a high-powered tycoon, you don't know much about delegating responsibilities." She turned away and dished up a bowl of scrambled eggs and thrust the bowl at Challon. "You go sit down and get out of my way while I finish up," she ordered briskly, as she turned back to the stove.

"May I help you?" Sheena asked politely. "I'm afraid I haven't had much practice in cooking, but I could do the donkey work."

The older woman shook her curly brown head firmly. "All we need is two inexperienced cooks in the kitchen. Tomorrow you'd probably be back in bed with a stomach ache, and I'd have *him* storming all over the place again." She turned the bacon carefully. "Knowleton may bow out as his personal physician as it is. He wasn't at all pleased with all that shouting and ranting."

To her surprise Sheena noted a guilty flush on Challon's face. "I was worried," he said belligerently, then took Sheena's arm again. "We'd better do as she says, or the shrew will probably poison us."

It wasn't until they were seated at the table before the fire and Challon had poured each of them a cup of coffee from the carafe on the sideboard, that he spoke again. "Laura isn't as tough as she pretends. Though, at times she comes pretty close. She's the most loyal individual I've ever known, but you've got to take the tart with the sweet where Laura's concerned."

Sheena stirred her coffee slowly, her eyes on the tall woman bustling briskly about the kitchen. "She doesn't look like my idea of a nanny. She's not exactly cozy, is she?"

Challon shook his head. "No, she's certainly not cozy. I wouldn't have known what to do with your standard model nanny when I was a kid. She would have been as out of place at Crescent Creek as Mary Poppins."

"Crescent Creek?" Sheena asked. She vaguely remembered that Barbara O'Daniels had mentioned that as one of Challon's assets.

"It's a ranch in the Rio Grande valley," he explained casually, leaning back in his chair. "I was born and raised there. My father made Crescent Creek his headquarters until my mother died when I was three. After that, he spent most of his time in Houston and only came home periodically."

"He didn't take you with him?" she asked, surprised.

Challon shook his head, "My father was definitely not the paternal type," he said dryly. "Not that I can blame him for not wanting to be saddled with me. I was a wild young hellion even then, and I didn't improve much as I got older. I nearly drove Laura crazy until I went away to college. She said that going back to teaching was a rest cure after raising me."

Sheena could well imagine the challenge that the young Rand Challon had offered.

"I'm surprised you didn't try to persuade her to stay on in some other capacity," Sheena said thoughtfully. It was clear that there existed a deep bond of affection between the two, and judging by her own experience with Challon's autocratic possessiveness, it was inconceivable that he would let her go easily.

He scowled. "I offered her everything from the position of housekeeper to a vice-presidency at Challon Oil, but she wouldn't stay. She said she wouldn't have a job created for her once she'd outlived her usefulness."

Evidently his failure to get his own way still rankled, for his lips tightened grimly. "Lord save me from an independent woman!"

Sheena smothered a tiny smile and looked quickly down at her coffee. So the arrogant Rand Challon didn't get his own way quite all of the time.

The affectionate rapport between Challon and Laura Bradford was not particularly obvious, Sheena noticed, when the older woman finished serving and joined them for breakfast a few moments later. Their conversation was light and bantering and on Laura's part tinged with acid tartness. It was only when Sheena watched closely that she saw the glimmer of tender amusement in Challon's eyes and the occasional fleeting expression of fierce, almost maternal pride on Laura Bradford's face as she looked at Rand Challon.

After breakfast, Challon's former governess banished them both firmly from the kitchen with an authority that caused Sheena to smile. Perhaps if Laura Bradford had stayed on, Rand Challon would not be quite the dictator he was today.

Perhaps Challon's meekness was due to the fact that the governess's orders had been in accordance to his own wishes, for he strode briskly to the closet in the foyer with Sheena firmly in tow. "You haven't been out of the house in a week. We'll get a little fresh air and some exercise."

He bundled her into a heavy green plaid jacket and pulled a red sock cap over her hair and ears. "You won't need boots any longer. Most of the snow has melted, and the little that's left refroze last night and is pretty hard packed."

"Snow?" Sheena asked. She dimly remembered that he'd mentioned on the night of their arrival that snow was expected. Strange to think that she'd been oblivious for an entire week to everything that wasn't contained within the four walls of that bedroom at the top of the stairs.

Challon had pulled on his sheepskin jacket now. "We

had one hell of a snowstorm," he said, as he grabbed her hand and opened the front door. "Knowleton almost didn't make it here." He grinned. "He said that he was going to bill me double for hazard pay."

The air was cold and sharp and felt marvelously invigorating as they made their way briskly down the hill, past the landing strip toward the woods beyond.

"This is really magnificent country," Sheena said, her gaze encompassing the majesty of the snowcapped mountains under a sky so blue that it hurt the eyes to behold.

"Wait a bit," Challon said, his eyes twinkling. "You haven't seen anything yet, little dove."

As they entered the forest, she was suddenly aware of what he meant. "It's beautiful," Sheena breathed ecstatically.

It was more than that, it was an enchanted fairyland from a distant childhood dream. The green pine trees were hung with countless garlands of icicles, which sparkled in the strong morning sunlight like multifaceted diamonds, their shimmering prisms reflecting their rainbow hues against the brilliant blue of the sky. The pristine blanket of snow crunched crisply beneath their feet as Challon led her down the winding trail to the small lake at the bottom of the hill. The lake was lent a breathtaking beauty by the winter's storm; the sparkling blue surface was coated with a thin sheet of ice that had a glittering transparency.

"It's as if a wicked magician imprisoned all this beauty for himself in his crystal ball," Sheena said softly.

"Trust the Irish to be lyrical about a natural phenomenon," Challon teased. "What really happened was that the lake froze solid and is now in the process of thawing."

Sheena smiled at him. "I like my explanation better. You Americans have no appreciation for the mystical."

"Remember that you're half American yourself," Challon pointed out, as he took her hand in his and stuck them both in his jacket pocket. "If your parents hadn't been killed when they were, you might even have gone there to live." They were strolling leisurely along the path that circled the lake, and Sheena found that she was enjoying the companionable intimacy of their walk.

Challon looked down at her. "Watch what you say about Americans, dove. You may live to regret it. I intend to deluge that Irish side of you so thoroughly with everything American that in six months time you'll be singing the 'Star-spangled Banner' instead of those dreary dirges you're so fond of."

Sheena chuckled. "You may succeed at that," she said lightly. "You've already got me wearing red, white, and blue."

He looked down at her blue jeans and the scarlet and white ski sweater revealed by her open coat and grinned. "I told you that I only had to sit back and let your own instincts take over in order to reform you. You're halfway there already, my fine Irish colleen."

She threw him an indignant look but still left her hand enveloped in his. She was too content to argue with him this morning. The sky was too blue, the crisp cold air too exhilarating, their surroundings too magically beautiful to spoil by conflict of any sort.

They had reached the upper end of the lake when Challon noticed Sheena's growing breathlessness. He stopped abruptly, his keen gaze raking her face and noting a faint flush on her cheeks. "You're getting tired. Why didn't you tell me that this was all too much for you? You're just out of a sickbed, for God's sake!"

She smiled involuntarily as she recalled how he had bustled her out of the house without even giving her a chance to say yea or nay. "I'm just a little tired. I didn't want to stop. It's so beautiful here, just give me a minute to catch my breath."

"Right," he said briskly. Ignoring her startled protest, he lifted her in his arms and strode swiftly to a fallen pine tree several yards away. He sat down on the log and cradled her in his lap. He opened his sheepskin coat and pulled her into its sheltering folds. "So rest, already."

Sheena wondered helplessly how he expected her to relax with her ear pressed to his hard, strong shoulder and the clean, earthy smell of him surrounding her. "This isn't necessary," she protested in a muffled voice as his hand began to stroke her tousled dark curls soothingly.

His chuckle reverberated in her ear. "No, but it's a hell of a lot of fun. Now lay still and let me cuddle you. It seems like a long time since I held you like this."

It had only been one night, she thought, but she wasn't in the mood to quibble at the moment. She was finding the warm, virile strength of Challon's body a heady contrast to the crisp coldness that surrounded them, and she unconsciously snuggled closer. She heard his low laugh again, this time with a note of triumph, and his arms tightened about her.

She could see his smoky breath on the still, cold air above her as he said, "You're like a fine-boned kitten, all softness and silk. And you're all mine, aren't you, love?"

She raised her head to protest, to tell him no, to tell him that she was no one's possession. But she met the golden intensity of his eyes, and the words died away without being spoken. There was no arrogant superiority, no smug triumph in his face at that moment. There was only a joyousness and a depth of tenderness that was incredible.

"Just as I'm completely yours," Challon said huskily, and slowly bent his head to take her lips.

Sheena felt her throat tighten with unshed tears at the sheer beauty of the moment. She lifted her hand unconsciously to stroke the hard contour of his cheek. It was cold beneath her fingers. But his lips were warm and coaxing as they brushed across her throat to rest against the pulse in the soft hollow.

"You're beginning to realize that now, aren't you, love?" he said softly. "You're beginning to know that I'd never take anything from you without giving a more than even exchange." His warm lips were on hers once more, and she could feel her heart stop in her throat at the glowing tenderness of his embrace. "Give to me," he urged softly. "Open to me, dove. Let me love you, and I promise that you'll never want to fly away again. Can't you feel that you've come home at last?"

She did feel it. But how did Challon know that she had been thinking just that as he wooed her with gentle lips and golden, magical words? Even though his words hinted of total bodily commitment, she felt no threat. It was somehow supremely natural to be lying languidly in his arms while he told her of the sexual commitment that was to be the next step in their relationship.

The next step. Suddenly she was jarred out of the golden haze that Challon had woven about her with his mesmerizing tenderness. So insidious had been his approach that she had not even been conscious of the giant inroads he had made in her resistance in a few short minutes. He had not even had to use that blindingly magnetic sexuality to bring her to the point of near surrender. He had merely to employ that coaxing gentleness, and she had been willing to give him anything he asked of her. And what he was asking of her was much more frightening than just a passionate interlude. He wanted to change her, mold her to his way of thinking. He was attempting to undermine the loyalties and responsibilities that were the lodestones about which her life revolved.

"No!" The cry startled Challon into a temporary loosening of his embrace. "No! I won't let you do this to me." She leaped to her feet and ran from him with a desperation that was all the more pronounced because of the chilly loneliness that she felt away from his arms. Her panic mounted in quantum leaps as she sped through the forest. By the time she had reached the cabin and flown up the steps and in the front door, her breathlessness was due as much to a wild sense of urgency as it was to her pell-mell flight up the hill.

She burst into the kitchen with an explosiveness that caused Laura Bradford to look up in startled amazement from the vegetables she was peeling at the sink.

"You've got to help me get away from here!" Sheena demanded. "Do you hear me? I've got to get away from here right now!"

Laura Bradford's keen brown eyes noted and comprehended Sheena's flushed face and the desperation in the wide, dark eyes, before looking back down at the potatoes she was peeling. "You're out of breath," she said calmly. "Sit down and relax a bit. There's no sense in getting yourself all upset for nothing."

"I don't want to sit down!" Sheena shouted. "I want to leave here. Don't you understand? I've been kidnapped, and I want you to help me leave this place!"

Laura Bradford glanced up, a grim smile on her face. "The boy's been rushing you, hasn't he?" she asked. "He never could wait when he wanted something."

"That 'boy' has committed a very serious crime," Sheena bit out, her dark eyes flaring. "You're obviously a woman of high ethical standards. You can't possibly approve of his actions, much less actually act as his accomplice."

The older woman gazed at Sheena's distraught face for a long moment before she picked up another potato and began peeling it carefully. "You're wrong," she said quietly. "I'd probably help him even if he asked me to commit murder." She looked up swiftly at Sheena's disbelieving gasp. "I'd do it in a minute," she said gruffly. "Because I'd know that Rand had a damn good reason for asking me to do it. I've known that boy almost all his life. If he took you against your will, he must have good cause. You'll get no help from me."

"Good cause!" Sheena cried, running her hand distractedly through her wild tangle of curls. "He sees me perform at a concert and decides it would be amusing to disrupt my entire life. I'd hardly call a spoiled playboy's whim good cause!"

"Now you just settle down," Laura said tersely. "Rand doesn't operate that way. He's never had a so-called 'whim' in his life. Even as a child he knew exactly what he wanted, and when he got it, he wasn't like other children, who grew bored and careless of their possessions. No matter how long Rand had something, it never lost its value for him."

Sheena shook her head dazedly. "You're as daft as he is," she said faintly. "You act as if I should be honored that he chose me to abduct."

Laura wiped her hands on a towel on the drainboard and turned to face Sheena. "I'm not saying that I approve of his methods, but you're right in thinking that I believe you don't realize your luck. Rand is very cautious about getting too close to anyone." Her lips curved bitterly. "He learned early that caring for anyone can hurt damnably. His father never cared for anyone or anything but that precious business empire of his." Her brandy-colored eyes flickered with a glint of the same toughness that Sheena had glimpsed in Challon's. "Well, for some crazy reason he cares about you. I've never seen him feel that same way about another woman. So if he wants you, I'm going to try my damndest to see that he gets you!"

"Just like that?" Sheena asked faintly, her eyes wide with shock. "You don't care what I feel, just so the great Rand Challon gets what he wants."

"That pretty well covers it," the former governess said. Then a glint of sympathy appeared in her eyes. "Why don't you just relax and let yourself flow with the tide?" she asked gently. "Rand is a fine man, and he really cares about you. Believe me, this isn't a flash in the pan for him."

"How can you know that?" Sheena asked bitterly. "You can't describe this as exactly normal behavior even for your fair-haired boy."

Laura Bradford bit her lower lip undecidedly and

then abruptly made up her mind. She moved forward swiftly and grasped Sheena firmly by the arm. "Come with me. I think it's time you saw something."

Laura ushered the younger woman out of the kitchen and down the hall. She threw open a door and stood aside to let Sheena precede her. "This is Rand's study," she announced. "I think it may hold a few surprises for you."

Sheena cast her a confused glance as she slowly entered the room. Rand's study was a small room carpeted in variegated rust shades. It contained a minimum of furniture: there was a small portable bar in one corner, a brown leather, tufted visitor's chair, and against the far wall a pine rolltop desk with papers stuffed in every pigeonhole.

But it wasn't the decor that caused Sheena to freeze in the center of the room and her mouth to drop open in shock. It was the pictures. There were pictures everywhere. Framed pictures on the walls and on the desk. Snapshots stuck in odd corners of the desk and one large colored photograph that had a place of honor on the wall above the desk.

"They're all of me," Sheena whispered dazedly, as she moved forward to stand before the desk. "But why?"

"Why do you think?" Laura Bradford asked tartly. "I should think it's fairly obvious that the man is obsessed by you."

Obsessed. Challon had used that word, too, Sheena thought, as her gaze remained glued to the wall above the desk. "The large color photograph is the one that appeared on the cover of the Paris *Match*," she said bewilderedly. "That was over two years ago." She shivered suddenly as she recognized her own strained and tragic face portrayed in black and white in a newspaper photo. "That was taken outside the hospital in Ballycraigh five years ago," she murmured huskily. She rubbed her head absently with one hand as if she could banish the clouds of bewilderment that were perplexing her. She touched another snapshot that was stuck in the corner of one of the framed photographs on the desk. "This one was taken before my parents died. I was only eight years old. I can understand how he could get hold of the other photos, but how on earth could he possibly have obtained this one?"

"I imagine his methods wouldn't bear looking into closely," Laura said dryly. "I do know that he's received a detailed report on you from a private detective agency every week for the past five years."

"Five years?" Sheena repeated stupidly. She couldn't comprehend the evidence of her own eyes much less the rest of what Laura Bradford had revealed. "That's completely incredible."

The older woman shrugged. "Perhaps. But it isn't really unusual when you know Rand Challon. As I told you, he always knows what he wants, and he never changes his mind. You'd be wise to accept that premise, first, if you ever expect to understand him."

"I've got to think," Sheena said, as she moved slowly toward the door. "None of this makes sense." As if she were sleepwalking, she passed Laura Bradford and headed for the stairs. "I've got to think," she repeated distractedly.

Laura Bradford followed her to the staircase and watched with narrowed eyes as she climbed the steps. "You do that," she said gruffly. "And while you're at it, you just might consider how rare it is to find a man who will cherish *anything* for that long in this day and age."

To her surprise Sheena was left alone for the rest of the day, due much to the influence of Laura Bradford, she suspected. Challon was not a man to rest on his laurels, and after that hour in the woods, she had expected him to approach her immediately to further consolidate the gains he had made. She was only grateful that he had been persuaded to give her the time she so desperately needed to retrieve a little of the equilibrium, which Laura Bradford's revelations had toppled.

She spent most of that afternoon sitting on the red tartan, cushioned window seat staring blindly out at the snowcapped mountains in the distance. Her mental processes were in such a state of upheaval that at first it was as if she were stunned. She evidently had completely misread the situation when she had believed that Challon's obsession for her was temporary and would vanish when he became bored with his game.

If Challon had not grown bored in five years of in-depth investigation, it was unlikely that she would be able to persuade him to release her in the few weeks that she had allotted herself for her holiday. She couldn't even begin to fathom the reasons behind those years of close surveillance, and toward evening she gave up even trying.

She stood up from the window seat and stretched wearily. She would shower and change, then go down to face Challon with her questions. She was certainly not getting anywhere with her own surmises.

She had just slipped a crimson velvet robe from a hanger in the closet and was on her way to the bathroom when there was a knock on the door.

Sheena bit her lip in vexation. She wasn't ready to face either Challon or Laura Bradford at the moment. She needed more time to erect her defenses and prepare the queries that must be asked. She sighed in resignation as she realized that neither Challon nor Laura Bradford would be put off by any protests or evasions on her part. She crossed the room swiftly and opened the door.

Rand Challon stood in the doorway with a covered tray in his hands and a hint of annoyance in his lion eyes. "It's about time," he said impatiently, as he pushed past her into the room. "I've brought your supper. You've had enough time to settle the question of world disarmament this afternoon. I told Laura that I wasn't about to give you any more time to brood, despite her tender concern for your feelings."

Sheena avoided his eyes, suddenly shy under the golden aggressiveness in his. "You needn't have gone to the trouble," she said quietly. "I was just going to shower and come downstairs."

"Well, now you won't have to bother," Challon said flatly. "Run along and take your shower. Your meal will still be warm when you're finished." He put the tray on the window seat and dropped down beside it.

He had changed from the jeans and wool sweater he had worn earlier, she noticed. He was now wearing suede rust pants that revealed the muscular strength of his thighs. The sleeves of his cream chambray shirt were rolled up to the elbow, and he had carelessly left a few buttons open, exposing his bronze muscular chest and a thatch of tawny hair.

He frowned impatiently as she stood gazing at him hesitantly. "You needn't look at me as if I'm some sort of Bluebeard," he said tersely. "Laura meant well, but I could have told her you weren't ready to hear it yet." He leaned back against the alcove wall and propped one foot on the window seat. "Well, it's done now. We'll talk after you've eaten."

So much for her plans of facing Challon in the more impersonal surroundings of the living room, Sheena thought. With his usual decisiveness, he was again molding the situation to suit himself.

"I'll only be a few moments," she said quietly, turning and walking once more toward the bathroom.

It was only slightly longer than that when she returned, but he'd had time enough to draw the drapes at the window and to build a fire in the fireplace. The tray was now on the hearth, and Challon was sprawled lazily on the chaise longue, looking ridiculously out of place on the distinctly feminine couch.

Challon looked up as she came through the door, and a smile lit his face as his gaze ran over her lingeringly. "I like you in that," he said softly. "I knew when I chose it that you'd look like a wild gypsy lass when you wore it."

"You chose it yourself?" she asked, looking down at the crimson velvet robe. It was a lushly extravagant garment with its low, square neckline and full, loose sleeves. The bodice was fitted, pointing up the slimness of her waist, and the skirt flared to lavish fullness. It was buttoned down the front, and there must have been a hundred tiny velvet-covered buttons from neckline to hem. It had taken her forever to fasten it.

Challon nodded. "I chose all of the clothes here," he said, rising to his feet. "You'll also find a complete wardrobe in my apartment in Houston and still another at Crescent Creek."

"How very extravagant of you," Sheena said lightly, as she came toward him. "I hope you made sure they were all returnable."

"Nope. They're all here to stay." He bent down and retrieved the tray from the hearth. "Just as you are, little dove." He gestured toward the chaise longue. "I think that you'd better sit there. It makes me feel like a female impersonator doing a Camille skit."

Sheena chuckled as she sat down. "You did look a bit uncomfortable," she told him. Her dark eyes were twinkling as he placed the tray on her lap and lifted off its cover.

"While you look just right," he said contentedly, as he sat down on the carpet at her feet. He pulled up his knees and rested his chin upon them, his golden eyes watching her gravely as she picked up her fork and started on the vegetable casserole. "It just goes to prove what a perceptive man I am."

She sighed resignedly. "Don't tell me you chose all the furnishings in this room, too."

"I'm afraid so," he admitted. "It got to be a kind of game. Buying things that I thought you'd enjoy and then imagining you using them. When I took a break last year and came up here, I even slept in your bed. I used to lie there with only the fire to illuminate the darkness and look at the portrait of Keane's dark-eyed waif above the mantel and think about my own waif."

Sheena's eyes flew to the portrait on the wall. The picture Challon painted was touchingly evocative, and she could feel her throat tighten helplessly. "But I'm not a waif," she protested huskily. "I have Uncle Donal."

Challon's lips tightened. "Yes, you have your uncle," he said curtly. "Which makes the description even more valid."

It was clear that no amount of reasoning was going to alter Challon's opinion of Donal O'Shea. "You were something of a waif yourself according to Miss Bradford," Sheena pointed out quietly.

He shrugged, "Laura has a very sentimental heart under that tough exterior. I was too wild to really miss the influence of a doting father. We never understood each other. He couldn't comprehend why I didn't want to follow in his footsteps. Challon Oil was the end-all of everything to my father."

He shrugged, his lips curving in a cynical smile. "After college, I batted around the world for awhile. I was a ski instructor one season at Saint Moritz. I joined a marine exploratory ship in the Caribbean for six months." His eyes were reminiscent. "I had a dozen jobs in those two years, but nothing my father would term gainful employment. Then I enlisted in the army and was sent to Vietnam." He got up abruptly and knelt before the fire with his back to her. Taking a poker from the andirons set, he stirred the fire briskly. "The army decided they had at last found my true vocation," he said bitterly. "They decided that I had the true killer instinct, and I was assigned to a special guerrilla corps. They were right. I was very good at it." He put the poker back on the stand and turned back to face her.

Sheena drew in her breath sharply as she saw his face. There was a stony ruthlessness that was almost primitive in the graven lines of his face, and the golden eyes were narrowed to the deadly gleam of a stalking puma.

He shook his head as if to clear it. As he met her wide, frightened eyes, the savagery gradually faded from his expression, and his lips twisted. "I came back from Nam with a truckload of medals, and everyone said that I was a changed man. They were right. I was changed, but not the way they thought."

He drew his legs up and once more leaned his chin on his knees, his eyes brooding into space. "I'd had a bellyful of war and killing and the whole miserable circus. I swore that once I got out of that uniform that I'd never do one damn thing that didn't bring me at least a modicum of pleasure and satisfaction." His voice roughened with sudden passion. "Life should be a celebration, for God's sake! Not a damn slaughterhouse." His lips curved in a bitter smile. "My father never understood that when I joined Challon Oil I was doing exactly what I wanted to do, and not assuming my dutiful responsiblities. I found out that I got a tremendous kick out of boardroom politics. It was even more fun than downhill racing. It was my killer instinct, I suppose." He shrugged. "My father died a happy man thinking that his erring son had at last seen the light." For a moment there was a poignant silence in the room that Sheena found impossible to break.

He grinned suddenly. "I didn't mean to lay my life story on you," he said lightly. "I just thought you had a right to know something about me, since turnabout is only fair play."

"That's very generous of you," Sheena said dryly. "But I don't think your report was quite as detailed as the ones you've received on me."

"You're quite right," Challon said, his golden eyes twinkling. "I didn't want to sully your delicate little ears with my more scandalous exploits." He got lithely to his feet. "Are you through with this?" he asked, gesturing to the tray.

Sheena nodded absently, and he removed it from her

lap and placed it on the hearth. He returned to sit down beside her on the chaise longue and take her hand in his. "All right, little dove, I'm now at your disposal. Fire away!"

Sheena found it hard to think as he lifted her hand and kissed the palm lingeringly, his tongue teasing her sensitive flesh. "You have the tiniest hands," he said. She could feel the vital heat of his body as he settled himself closer to her.

She drew a deep, shaky breath. "You know all the questions," she said huskily. "Suppose you just furnish me with the answers."

"Fair enough." His hands were idly playing with her fingers as he said, "I saw a picture of you in a newspaper at the time of your brother's death five years ago. It moved me more than anything that I'd ever known. Your face seemed to encompass all the sadness and weariness in the world." He frowned at the memory. "It made me mad as hell. For some reason, I felt as if someone had damaged something that belonged to me." He shook his head ruefully. "I thought I was going crazy. I kept seeing your face and remembering those big black eyes until I found myself searching the newspapers for any news of you. It was like a compulsion. I finally decided that the only way to get you out of my mind was to find out as much as I could about you and remove the mystique."

"That's when you hired the detective agency," Sheena guessed.

He nodded. "Right. But it didn't accomplish the purpose that I intended it to. Instead of dissipating the fascination I felt for you, it magnified it. The reports began to be an accepted part of my week, and it became a positive passion to know every nuance of your life. I even had the detective take photos of you as you went about your daily schedule. Those photographs in the study are quite meager compared to the lot I have at Crescent Creek." He lifted her hand to nibble delicately at her fingers. "I sometimes thought I'd gone completely haywire. You were only seventeen then, and I was almost twenty-nine. I alternated between my desire to meet you, and the knowledge that I had no business in your life until you were older and more capable of handling everything I was going to ask of you." He looked up and smiled lovingly into her bemused face. "I knew even then that I was going to ask a hell of a lot from you, dove." He looked down at her hand again. "You never wear jewelry," he observed inconsequentially. "Don't you like it?"

"Not particularly," Sheena answered. "I wear earrings occasionally."

"I'd like to see you in those golden dangly things," he said. "I love you with that wild gypsy look."

"You thought you were too old for me?" she prompted impatiently, anxious to get him back on the track.

"What?" he asked vaguely. "Oh, yes. Well, I decided that I could give you the time you needed as long as I knew there wasn't anyone else in the wings. Thanks to dear Uncle Donal, I didn't have to worry about possible rivals. He protected you just as jealously as I would have myself." His lips were brushing against her fragile, blue-veined wrist. "As the years passed, I developed the joys of anticipation to a fine art. Sometimes it was rather like a Chinese water torture to have you so much a part of my life and yet not be able to see or touch you." His tongue touched the rapid pulse in her wrist, and she jerked it away, tucking her hand beneath the folds of her robe. She found she was liking his light, teasing lovemaking far too much.

He gave her a knowing, satisfied glance. "I thought I was giving you ample time to get over your brother's death and grow up a little, but thanks to O'Shea, it didn't work out that way." His hand was now stroking a fold of the soft velvet robe. He was evidently a very tactile man, Sheena thought absently.

"I was going to give you until the end of the year before I came over to Ireland to get you. But then O'Shea arranged your American tour, and I couldn't resist going to see you. Needless to say, that accelerated my plans somewhat." He smiled. "I should have known that I wouldn't be able to resist taking you, sweetheart. I'd waited far too long already."

"So you just kidnapped me," Sheena said blankly. "You decided that you wanted me, and you just took me." She snapped her fingers. "Just like that."

He shook his tawny head, his golden eyes oddly grave. "You haven't been listening, dove. I don't deny that I want you, but that's not the reason I abducted you."

"Then why?" she asked bewilderedly.

"I love you," he said simply .

Sheena could feel the blood drain from her face as her eyes widened with shock. "You couldn't love me," Sheena protested. "You don't even know me."

"I know more about you than most men know about their wives on their golden wedding anniversaries," he said. "And everything I know, I love. I know that there's tenderness and mischief lying in wait beneath that solemn face you wear. I know you have a temper that makes you look like a stormy child on occasion. I know that you're a passionate gypsy of a woman just waiting to come alive."

She stared as if mesmerized as he swiftly leaned forward and lifted her to the far side of the chaise longue. "Scoot over, love." He slid up to rest his head on the back of the chair, his body turned facing her. The confines of the chaise longue brought them in sudden breathless proximity.

He chuckled as his arms went around her and he pulled her into his embrace. "I forgot to tell you that this was another one of my fantasies," he said. "That was why I made sure this chaise longue was very, very roomy."

His lips hovered for a teasing moment over her own before closing with a slow sensuousness that caused her to arch against him and to open her lips to the sweet invasion of his tongue. "That's right, love, open to me. Let me come into every part of you. God, I want you!"

His lips were taking her feverishly now, moving over the silky flesh of her throat with a hunger that was almost savage in its intensity. She arched her throat, as if to the kiss of the sun. Then she felt his hands at the tiny buttons on the bodice of the robe. He had already undone four of the buttons when she was moved to protest.

She put a restraining hand on his busy fingers, and he looked up. "It's all right, dove," he said, smiling lovingly as he perceived the dazed confusion on her face. He gently moved her hand aside and continued to unbutton the robe.

"Do you know that some desert tribesmen garb their brides in beautiful caftans with hundreds of buttons like these on their wedding nights? They say that each button is a step closer to paradise." His hands had reached the buttons at her waist now. "I thought of that the day I bought the robe."

He pushed her a little away from him and looked down at her, his face taut and hungry with need. "I love you," he said huskily. "Believe me when I say that I wouldn't do anything to hurt you." His hands slowly spread the robe open, his eyes fixed on her small, perfectly formed breasts with their pink-tipped crowns. "I know that you don't love me yet, but I can teach you. I think your body already loves me a little."

His head bent slowly, and his tongue teasingly encircled one taut nipple, which immediately hardened eagerly in response. "Oh, yes, your body loves me." His hands cupped her breasts gently while his teeth and tongue tormented the swollen nipples until Sheena cried out and clutched his head closer to her breasts in an agony of frustration.

He moved over her, one leg parting hers as his hands rhythmically squeezed her breasts and his tongue continued its play at her nipples. He slowly lowered his thighs so that she could feel his warm, hard arousal through the velvet of her robe. She gave a feverish gasp as his hips began a rhythmic thrusting movement that matched the tempo of his hands on her breasts.

She was writhing beneath him now, making tiny mewing noises, her hands clutching helplessly at his brawny shoulders. She had never experienced such a fever as was flooding every limb in her body and centering in the fluid apex of her loins. "Rand," she gasped, her head moving from side to side on the back of the chaise longue. "Rand."

His face above her was flushed and harsh with need, his eyes narrowed with tigerish pleasure as they watched each new sensation reflected in her face.

Suddenly his hands left her breasts, and he swung off her body with lithe swiftness. His breath was coming in labored jerks as he stood up and walked to the fireplace to stand with his back to her, staring into the flames.

Sheena sat up slowly, her dazed eyes on Challon's muscular shoulders, bent as if he were in pain. It had all happened so swiftly that she couldn't comprehend what had transpired. Her hands went automatically to the buttons of her bodice, and he must have heard her move, for he whirled to face her.

He took one look at her bewildered face and the pained darkness in her eyes and swiftly crossed back to her and dropped down beside her once more. "Poor little dove," he crooned tenderly, as his hand gently stroked her black curls. "It wasn't very fair to you, was it? Well, take comfort that it was pure hell for me to stop. I've never wanted anyone in my life the way I wanted you just now. But it's not enough, Sheena. We deserve more, and I'll be damned if we don't get it!"

"More?" she repeated dazedly. How could there possibly be more than the mind-jolting excitement that they had just experienced?

Challon nodded, his fingers absently threading through her curls. "More. You don't love me yet, but you will very soon. I think you care more than you know right now." He tilted her head back to kiss her with lingering sweetness, and she instinctively melted against him. "After five years, I can wait a little longer for it to be totally perfect." He drew a deep breath and put her firmly away from him. "Correction. I can wait, if I get the hell out of here."

He stood up reluctantly, his gaze running lingeringly over her pink, swollen lips and tousled black curls before moving down to her unbuttoned bodice. His hand reached out compulsively to caress one pert breast beneath the crimson velvet, his golden eyes darkening to amber. Then giving a sigh that was more like a shudder, he moved away from her and walked slowly to the door.

He turned, his hand on the knob, and even in the dimness of the flickering firelight, she could see the twinkle in his golden eyes. "We only made it halfway to paradise tonight," he said mockingly. "But be sure you keep that robe on hand, dove. I guarantee that we'll get there the next time."

Five

"You cheated!" Sheena accused, throwing her cards down in disgust. "I don't know why I play with you, Rand Challon. I must be some sort of masochist to take the kind of beating you hand out and still come back for more." She stood up and stretched lazily, like a small, sinuous cat. "Well, I won't be so foolish again. No one can be as lucky as that."

Rand leaned lazily back in his chair at the card table and began to gather the cards and stack them. His golden eyes were twinkling as he observed her stormy, indignant face and mutinous mouth. "I'm glad you finally realized that, dove," he drawled. "Anyone else would have tumbled to that particular bit of knowledge a week ago. I was beginning to think you were a little thick. You were a lamb ready for the fleecing, and I've never been known to stay my hand when the stakes are that tempting."

"You have the gall to admit it!" Sheena said, planting her hands on her hips and glaring at him fiercely. "Have you no ethics at all?"

"Not where you're concerned," Rand said blandly. "Now, come around here and pay up."

"I most certainly will not," she said haughtily. "All bets are off. You have your nerve even suggesting such a thing after confessing what a scoundrel you are."

"Scoundrel?" Challon cocked his tawny head inquiringly. "Lord, what an old-fashioned word. But I like the way it rolls off your tongue in that funny little brogue."

"Oh!" Sheena knotted her fists in frustration. "You're completely impossible. You have absolutely no sense of shame. I refuse to even speak to you." She whirled and marched across the room to the couch in front of the fireplace and plopped down indignantly.

She was hardly seated when she heard Challon push back his chair and stand up. "Actually, I prefer it that way, sweetheart," Rand said mischievously. "It saves so much time."

Before she had time to look over her shoulder, he was across the room and on the couch beside her. He gathered her swiftly up in his arms and transferred her into his lap. "Now, pay up," he ordered. "I've been waiting all evening for my just reward."

"Just reward?" Sheena said indignantly. "You have—" The rest of her protest was smothered beneath his lips. For fully thirty seconds she withstood temptation and kept her body stiff and unresponsive. Then as Challon deepened the kiss, she gave a low moan and melted against him as she always did. It was a feverish and breathless fifteen minutes before he reluctantly stopped kissing her. They were both flushed and shaken, and Sheena could hear Rand's heart beating furiously beneath her ear. She did not recall when she had unbuttoned his green-and-black-plaid shirt, but it was an uncontested fact that her face was pressed to the wiry mat of tawny hair on his chest. She moved her cheek in sensuous enjoyment, liking the feel of the roughness against the smoothness of her cheek. He always

THE RELUCTANT LARK • 79

smelled deliciously of clean soap and that warm earthy
odor that was distinctly his own.

"Be still," Rand growled, pressing her head firmly to
his chest. "These damn teasing petting sessions are
driving me up the wall. Do you know that I didn't sleep
until nearly dawn last night?"

Sheena refused to admit to him that she had been in
a similar state when they had parted the night before.
She had burned with an aching hunger that had caused
her to toss restlessly for hours.

"I'm certainly not forcing you to make love to me,"
she said tartly, making a motion to slip off his lap.

"Just be still," he ordered. "I'm well aware our present status quo is my own choice, but it doesn't make it
any easier when I have to let you go. Just give me a
minute to cool down."

She lay quietly in his arms, intimidated for the moment by the hunger in his voice.

She was fully aware that he was entirely correct in
his statement. She had admitted to herself some time
ago that Challon could have taken her anytime in the
last week, and she wouldn't have uttered a single protest.
She smiled ruefully as she realized what a gross
understatement that was. There had been moments in
this last week when she had been not only eager but
frantic for him to carry on with his lovemaking to its
final conclusion. Sometimes she had been in a positive
fury of frustration and had unconsciously tried to
tempt him into breaking that tightly leashed control,
but to no avail. Challon's steely determination had never
wavered, even in the face of that physical chemistry
that was like an electric force field surrounding them.

The past week had been the strangest one that Sheena
had ever known. Balanced on the fine edge of desire,
the days had still possessed a warm, tranquil
contentment. Challon had possessed every moment of
her waking day with a sweeping arrogance that she
found curiously comforting. There were no troublesome decisions to make because he made them for her,

and she had no option but to flow in Challon's turbulent wake. There were long walks every morning that she found highly enjoyable, hours of companionable conversation and equally companionable silences. In the afternoons they usually lunched with Laura Bradford and then played chess until time to change for dinner.

In the evenings Laura conveniently disappeared to her room after dinner, and then Challon had initiated Sheena into the intricacies of poker. Claiming that the game lacked zest with the gambling element removed, Challon had instituted forfeits into the game that were as heady as they were enjoyable. This inevitably led to their lingering in each other's arms until they could bear no more of the addictive caresses without committing their bodies totally.

Sheena unconsciously nestled closer to Challon's hard body as she remembered the heated pleasure he gave her so effortlessly. As she had noticed previously, he was a very tactile man, and even when he was not making love to her, he seemed to take great pleasure in just holding her hand or stroking her throat as he conversed lazily with her. She found she took equal pleasure in the cuddling and casual touching and found herself reaching out with equal eagerness to take his hand or tentatively touch the hard swell of the muscles in his forearm.

Sheena had never thought herself a particularly passionate woman, but Rand seemed to be able to set her on fire with only that curiously intimate smile or simply by running his fingers casually from the curve of her elbow to her wrist.

At times she wondered why she accepted her captivity with such passivity after her initial fury and indignation. She decided that the answer must lie in the odd sense of unreality that pervaded her stay in this beautiful place. The experience was so far removed from her ordinary life that it had a curious dreamlike quality. Everything, that is, but her relationship with

Rand Challon. Nothing could be more vividly real than this golden lion man, and he made sure that she was fully conscious of the fact.

"If you've gone to sleep on me, I'm going to be most annoyed with you, love." Challon's amused voice broke through her reverie. "It's bad enough trying to keep myself from sampling that lovely body of yours, without the very insulting knowledge that I've bored you to sleep!"

She had been vaguely aware of the gradual loosening of the hard tension of Rand's body and that his arms were now cuddling her with the almost sexless affection of a small boy with his favorite teddy bear.

"Oh, you managed to keep me awake," she said demurely, as she snuggled her head in her favorite hollow by his collarbone. "Barely."

She felt his chest vibrate as he chuckled. "God, you've gotten saucy. I can hardly recognize you as the shy little gypsy I snatched two weeks ago. You've got me reeling most of the time these days from one cause or another. Either it's that stinging nettle of a tongue or that delightfully passionate responsiveness."

"I haven't noticed any obvious lapse of control," she said, a hint of huffiness in her voice.

"That's because I'm a very devious fellow. I assure you that I've been walking on hot coals all week, but I wasn't about to let you have the benefit of my virile young body without being sure that you respected me. How could I know that you wouldn't just take me and cast me aside in the morning?"

Sheena gave a derisive snort that caused him to chuckle once again. Playing with her dark curls, he said softly, "But it won't be long now, dove. I can feel you coming closer to me all the time. You'll say the words I want to hear soon, won't you?"

She leaned back in his arms to regard him with troubled dark eyes. "I don't know," she whispered confidingly. "I'm so confused that I don't know what I'm feeling. I know that there's something between us that I've never felt before. But is that the emotion you're asking from me?"

There was a flicker of disappointment in the depths of Challon's eyes as he kissed her lightly on the nose. "I'm rushing things again," he said with forced lightness. "Take all the time you need, dove. I can wait." He pushed her off his lap and stood up. "Now, I'd better send you off to bed. I want you to be rested for tomorrow. We're going to have visitors."

"Visitors?" Sheena whirled to face him, her eyes wide with surprise.

Rand nodded, as he slipped his arm around her waist and propelled her gently toward the staircase. "My secretary, Marcy Lovett, is flying in with some contracts that I have to sign. I arranged for Dr. Knowleton to come at the same time to give you a final check-up. You've never gotten over that little cough you developed after your chill."

"But I feel fine," she protested. The knowledge of the sudden intrusion on their privacy disturbed her for some unknown reason. She had been aware that Challon was in constant radio contact with his home base. She supposed she should have known that a powerful economic figure such as Challon could not remain isolated for long from his business interests, yet she was experiencing an odd dissatisfaction at the thought that she must now share Challon's attention with his work. "Aren't you afraid that I might appeal to your secretary or Dr. Knowleton to rescue me?" she asked tartly, tossing her head. "Or have you bought their loyalty, too?"

Challon shook his head, a frown darkening his face. "Some people can't be bought. But," he added with deliberate ruthlessness, "they can be destroyed. I don't think you'd want to put me in a position of having to defend myself." His lips twisted bitterly. "The killer instinct, remember?"

Sheena shivered involuntarily as she remembered his granite-hard face that evening in the firelight. No, she would hesitate to expose anyone to that brutally dangerous side of Rand Challon.

Rand noticed the involuntary withdrawal, for he immediately set about restoring her confidence and compliance in a way that was both enjoyable and eminently successful. When he raised his head from her lips, he and Sheena were both flushed and breathing hard. "Don't ever be afraid of me, Sheena," he said quietly. "I'll never be a threat to you. On the contrary, my entire resources will always be available to protect you and make your way smoother."

"Except when you decide otherwise," she murmured, a spark of mischief in her enormous black eyes. "I don't know whether to trust you or not, Rand Challon. Tonight you revealed your true colors. You had no compunction at all about cheating a poor, naive Irish lass. How do I know you won't do it again?"

Challon grinned. "I'm a reasonably honest man unless the temptation is totally irresistible. And you happen to be the only prize that constitutes that much of a challenge for me. Besides, now that you're on to my tricks, I wouldn't dare try to manipulate you, dove."

Sheena regarded his innocent expression and dancing golden eyes suspiciously. "You'd dare anything," she stated flatly. "And you were entirely too good at your 'tricks' to be a complete novice. Where did you learn to cheat at cards, Rand?"

"Well, now that you mention it, there was a time in my disreputable past when I was a blackjack dealer at a casino in Nassau."

"Rand Challon, you're a black-hearted rogue with no principles whatever! Have you no scruples at all? I trusted you!"

"You can always trust me in anything important, dove. I just decided that in this particular wager, it would be to our mutual advantage for me to emerge the victor. Now, up you go. I can feel my willpower eroding very rapidly."

He turned her around and started her up the steps

with a firm slap on her derriere. "I'll see you at break-fast at eight. The plane won't be here until ten, so we'll have time for our walk before Knowleton and Marcy arrive. Sleep well, dove."

The Lear jet was descending with the screaming grace of a predatory eagle when Sheena and Challon emerged from the woods and made their way leisurely toward the runway where the jet would touch down. By the time the sleek, streamlined bird had rolled to a stop, they were standing waiting by the hangar.

As the passenger door opened and the automatic steps emerged, Sheena waited with a tinge of curiosity for her first sight of Rand's secretary. Whenever he had mentioned Marcy Lovett in the past week, it had been with respect and admiration, and Sheena had received an impression of a superefficient dynamo with computerlike accuracy.

The woman who came hurrying down the steps looked more like a college girl than the paragon of Challon's description. Dressed in buttercup yellow pants and ski jacket, Marcy Lovett was a tall, slim woman with short, curly brown hair and a turned-up nose that was liber-ally dusted with freckles. Her hazel eyes were apprehen-sive as she hastily crossed the tarmac to stand before Challon, and there was a sheepish smile on her pleas-ant face. "You're going to murder me," she announced, grimacing. "But, so help me God, I couldn't help it. The woman practically shanghaied me."

"Simmer down, Marcy," Rand said. "Who shanghaied you?"

Marcy Lovett cast an uncomfortable glance at Sheena, her gaze moving down to Challon's large hand linked with Sheena's. "Donna Scott," she finally said reluctantly. "I did everything I could to deter her, but the woman is a positive bloodhound. She's been on your trail for over three months, and I don't know how she found out I was coming here today."

"I hope you're not saying what I think you're saying," Rand said, his voice dangerously soft. "You brought her with you?"

Marcy Lovett nodded unhappily. "I told you that you were going to murder me. But there was no way I could get out of it, short of pushing her out of the plane without a parachute. She was already at the airport when I arrived this morning at five." She distractedly ran her hand through her short, curly hair. "I didn't think glamour girls like her ever got up before noon. God, I'm sorry, Rand."

"It's okay," Rand said. "I'll take care of it. I know how determined Donna can be when she zeroes in on something. Where is she now?"

"She and Dr. Knowleton are still on the plane." The secretary grimaced. "She wouldn't get off until she repaired the ravages of the trip on that beautiful face, and Dr. Knowleton wouldn't leave her side. She's been sharpening her technique on him since we left Houston." There was a definite note of warning in Marcy Lovett's voice.

"Donna has no more technique than a steamroller," Rand said dryly. "Someone told her as a child that persistence always wins the day, and she's subscribed to the maxim ever since. I suppose I'd better go rescue Knowleton before she makes him so dizzy he'll be useless to us."

He dropped Sheena's hand and started for the plane. "Take care of Sheena, Marcy."

Sheena bristled momentarily at this offhand dismissal, and she met Marcy Lovett's tentative smile with a distinctly cool one of her own.

"Look, I'm really sorry about this," the secretary said apologetically. "I didn't mean to bring that blond vamp down on both of you." She bit her lip worriedly. "Rand was so upset that he didn't bother to introduce us. I'm Marcy Lovett. I've been Rand's secretary for the past four years."

"How do you do," Sheena said politely. "I'm Sheena Reardon."

"Yes, I know," Marcy said frankly, smiling. "I think it's so romantic that you and Rand are back together again after all this time. I wouldn't have had anything spoil your reunion for worlds."

"Back together?" Sheena asked bewilderedly.

Marcy nodded. "I've been seeing your pictures ever since the day Rand hired me. I'm glad you've settled your differences and are a twosome again."

Sheena shook her head at the secretary's misconception. Marcy Lovett obviously thought that she and Rand had had a lover's quarrel and broken up before her arrival on the scene. It was a natural conclusion under the circumstances and far more believable than the true story. "Thank you," Sheena said. "You're very kind." Then unable to contain her curiosity any longer, she asked. "Who is Miss Scott?"

Marcy Lovett covered her mouth with her hand. "Oh, Lord, I was afraid you didn't know about her." She groaned. "I'll be lucky if I get out of this with my job intact." Her hazel eyes were earnest as she said comfortingly, "Don't worry, he hasn't seen Donna Scott in over four months. I'm sure that he's finished with her. She just thinks she's so irresistible that she can't believe it." She made a face. "The lady's IQ isn't nearly as devastating as her looks."

"And is she that irresistible?" Sheena asked slowly, her eyes on Challon's lean figure as he quickly crossed the tarmac.

"She's gorgeous," Marcy admitted reluctantly. "She's quite a famous model when she's not jetting around with the beautiful people." Then as her eyes caught a movement at the entrance at the top of the stairs, she added wryly, "It appears that you're about to be afforded the opportunity to judge for yourself. I believe Miss Scott has just finished gilding the lily."

Sheena wondered gloomily what Donna Scott could possibly have done that would have improved her already radiant appearance. Her sparkling white ski jacket with fox fur trim was cut with an understated elegance, and it clothed a tall, sleek figure that still was voluptuously curved. Her long, ash-blond hair was styled in a sophisticated pageboy that framed a depressingly perfect face. Her pansy blue eyes were glowing meltingly, and her lips were parted in a brilliant smile as she came toward Challon, her hands outstretched.

Sheena could not hear her words as she greeted Challon, but she could see that the woman's smile widened delightedly at Challon's reply. It seemed that Rand was not as angry at Donna Scott's arrival as Marcy believed, Sheena thought vexedly, as the ravishing blond pressed a warm kiss on Challon's lips before slipping her arm intimately through his.

Donna Scott and Challon had been joined by a thin, dapper man in his late forties, and the trio were now walking toward them.

Sheena bit her lower lip in annoyance as she noticed the way the model was clinging to Rand's arm and the look of indulgent amusement in Rand's eyes as he looked down at her vivacious face.

"Sheena, I'd like you to meet an old friend, Donna Scott," Rand said, as they reached the hangar. "This is Sheena Reardon, Donna." He clapped the slight, wiry man on the shoulder. "And this is Thad Knowleton. You've already met, but you've unfortunately found him very forgettable."

"A hazard of my profession," the doctor said wryly. His handshake was firm and his blue eyes both gentle and keen behind his horn-rimmed glasses. "You're looking very much better than the last time I saw you, Miss Reardon. How are you feeling?"

Challon frowned impatiently. "You can go into all that later, Thad. I want you to give her a thorough examination this afternoon. Laura should have brunch ready. Let's go on up to the cabin."

Sheena noticed that her own polite acknowledgment of the introduction to Donna Scott had been met with a vague nod and a pleasant smile that still managed to contain an almost childlike curiosity. "Have we met before?" she asked in a clear, bell-like tone that was oddly incongruous with her sultry appearance. "Rand and I have a number of the same friends. I'm sure that I've seen you somewhere."

"No, you haven't," Challon said emphatically, taking her arm and turning her firmly toward the path that led to the cabin.

Despite this assurance the model continued to give Sheena occasional puzzled glances over her shoulder as she climbed the hill to the cabin. In her indignant surprise, Sheena barely noticed that Rand had left her to trail behind with Marcy Lovett while he strode ahead with Knowleton and the gorgeous model on either side. She had grown used to Challon's exclusive attention, and she found it a trifle disconcerting to be so casually dismissed at the first appearance of these visitors from the outside world. Not that it mattered to her if an entire harem of Challon's old flames chose to drop in, she thought crossly.

Why should it bother her if instead of the dangerously exciting level of communication that she had become accustomed to, she was being treated with the amused indulgence that he might have displayed toward his favorite niece? After all, she had known that this crazy obsession Challon had for her would eventually fade in the light of reality. She had just not thought that reality would be embodied by the lush, provocative figure of one Donna Scott.

That the gorgeous blond was attracting Challon to her like a powerful magnet was evidenced over brunch. The model was sitting next to him, and he exerted a cosmopolitan charm on the entire company that was dazzling in its appeal. Sheena could not even recognize the man she had grown to know over the last two weeks in this sophisticated tycoon. His attitude toward her had undergone a complete metamorphosis in the time it had taken for his former mistress to get off the plane. Former mistress? Judging by the attention he was lavishing on the voluptuous Miss Scott, the relationship was very much in the present.

To her infinite frustration, she couldn't even find fault with Donna Scott. The woman was perfectly enchanting. It was obvious that Marcy was correct that the lovely Miss Scott wasn't overly bright, but she more than made up for it with an endearing little-girl air and almost effusive friendliness. Even Sheena received her share of the model's wide-eyed interest. An interest that Rand immediately deflected back to himself, she noticed grimly.

Sheena was more than eager to leave the table when Challon stood up and turned to Knowleton to say briskly, "Suppose you take Sheena up to her room and give her that examination now, Thad. I have to go over those contracts with Marcy." He checked the gold watch on his wrist. "I'd like to see you in my study in an hour, if that's convenient for you."

Knowleton nodded and rose leisurely to his feet. "That should give me plenty of time," he agreed. He cocked an eyebrow inquiringly at Sheena. "If you're ready, Miss Reardon?"

Sheena nodded, a stormy frown darkening her face. Even if she hadn't been very eager to escape from the dining room, she knew that Rand would have found a way of disposing of her troublesome presence. "I'm quite ready," she said icily, throwing her napkin down on the table.

"And what about me?" Donna Scott asked, her lips pursed in a provocative pout. She placed a perfectly manicured hand on Challon's arm caressingly. "You're surely not going to desert me after I've come all this way to see you. Can't those boring old contracts wait for a while, darling?"

Challon lifted the hand on his arm to his lips. "You're going to use my bedroom and take a nice long siesta," he said lightly, as he kissed her palm lingeringly. "You left Houston at a god-awful hour, and you must be exhausted. I want you well-rested when I get out from under this paperwork."

There was a wealth of meaning in the last sentence, and the gorgeous model responded with a smile filled with delight.

"I promise that you won't be disappointed," she said huskily, moistening her lips in sultry invitation. "You won't be long, Rand?"

He shook his head with an intimate smile that pledged as much as her own. "You know me better than that. When could I ever wait?"

Sheena felt an obscure sense of shock at the blatantly sexual overtones of that conversation. He might as well have boldly stated to the entire company how he intended on spending the rest of the afternoon. She felt suddenly violently sick to her stomach.

She pushed back her chair hurriedly. "If you'll excuse me," she muttered, jumping up and almost running from the room. She barely made it to her bathroom upstairs before she lost the meal she had just eaten. After she had brushed her teeth and bathed her face in cold water, she was a little better, but she still felt a little nauseated, and there was a queer throbbing ache in her breast. She must be coming down with something, she assured herself feverishly. Why else would she be swept up in this painful turmoil? She almost welcomed the soft knock that announced the arrival of Thad Knowleton.

Her relief was rapidly dissipated as the doctor proceeded to ask her to put on a robe and then gave her the most embarrassingly thorough physical she'd ever received. It was accompanied with a barrage of questions that caused the color to mount to her cheeks and remain through the entire interview. When he was finally satisfied, he sat back in the easy chair beside her bed and said, "You're very much improved, Miss Reardon. I have a few recommendations that I'll take up with Rand, but on the whole I couldn't be more pleased with your progress." He smiled. "I admit that I was a trifle concerned when you had to leave us so abruptly downstairs, but I'm sure it was just a temporary indisposition."

"I thought perhaps I might have a touch of the flu," Sheena suggested tentatively.

Thad Knowleton shook his head as he closed his bag and fastened it securely. "I think you'll find you're completely recovered very shortly," he said with a curious smile. "By tomorow at the latest." He stood up. "Well, it's time I presented myself in the study with my report." He smiled wryly. "Despite Rand's courteous phrasing, he fully expects me to be right on time with the information he wants from me. A very dynamic and demanding man, our Rand Challon." He moved toward the door. "I'll see you at dinner, Miss Reardon."

As the door closed behind him, Sheena sat up on the bed and zipped up her robe. She'd just swung her legs off the bed when there was a cursory knock and the door opened.

"I saw Thad leave, and I thought that we could have a little chat," Donna Scott said brightly, as she entered the room and closed the door behind her. She leaned against the door, looking enchantingly feminine in the pink satin wrapper that lovingly outlined her generous curves. "I got a little bored waiting for Rand." She made a little moue. "He has a habit of forgetting everything when business raises its ugly head." Her violet eyes darkened dreamily. "I don't really mind, I suppose. He always makes up for it when he does remember me."

Sheena felt a thrust of pain that nearly took her breath away. "I don't know what we have to discuss, Miss Scott," Sheena said quietly, feeling a twinge of nervous tension in the pit of her stomach. "And I really must go down and help Laura with the washing up."

"That will wait." Donna Scott moved toward the window seat and settled herself gracefully. "There's something I want to ask you."

Sheena sighed as she rose and crossed to lean against the brown easy chair. "Then I suppose you might as well go ahead with it." There was no chance the blond wouldn't do that anyway, she thought bitterly. She could see now why Rand compared her tactics to that of a steamroller. Not that the realization of her character had prevented him from inviting her to roll right over him.

Donna Scott crossed one lovely leg over the other and smiled sweetly. "I think you know why I'm here. I was Rand's mistress for over six months, and I intend to have him back. I want you to help me."

Sheena's lips dropped open in surprise. "Me?" she asked faintly, "You want me to help you?"

Donna Scott nodded eagerly. "I know you'll want to help Rand and me with our reconciliation after he's been so kind to you. He told me how he brought you here to recuperate after you became ill." Her lovely pansy eyes appraised Sheena's fragile form and frowned. "You're still dreadfully thin, aren't you?" Then her face cleared. "But Thad did say you were much better."

"Yes, much better," Sheena echoed numbly. So that was the excuse Challon had given his mistress for her presence in the cabin. She felt a knife-thrust of pain, and then a slow burning anger began to kindle.

"Then I'm sure you won't mind leaving a little earlier than you'd planned," Donna said complacently. When she caught Sheena's stunned expression, she rushed on. "Not that Rand and I wouldn't be happy to have you stay with us at some later time. Rand explained how close your two families have been over the years. It's just that right now we have a few differences to straighten out, and we need a little time alone together."

"I see," Sheena said, over the lump in her throat. "And have you discussed this with Rand?"

Donna shook her head. "Not yet, but I'm sure he'll agree." She smiled dreamily. "You saw the way he behaved at lunch. I'm sure he's missed me as much as I've missed him." Her face clouded with puzzlement. "I can't understand why he's been acting so peculiar lately. He knows how good we are together." Then she shrugged as if dismissing the subject. "Oh, well, he's obviously come to his senses at last." She rose gracefully to her feet and smiled entreatingly at Sheena. "Can I count on you, Sheena?"

"I'll think about it," Sheena said, forcing the words through lips that felt parched.

"Nassau would be a much healthier place for you to recuperate, don't you think?" Donna Scott said coaxingly. "I have some friends who have a lovely villa there. I'm sure they'd love to have you stay until you're really well."

"I said that I'd think about it," Sheena said between her teeth, her fists clenching at her sides. Oh, God, let her go away before I decide to strangle her. Physical action would probably be the only thing she would understand.

Donna Scott was absolutely incredible! Sheena had never seen anyone so blatantly self-centered and obstinate in her entire life. Yet she was convinced that Donna honestly believed that her demand was perfectly just and reasonable. What vanity and sunny denseness!

"Thank you, Sheena," she said. "I knew you would want to do the right thing, once you knew all the circumstances." She tightened the tie at the waist of her satin robe, and her luscious lips parted in a smile of satisfaction. "And now I'm going to go back to Rand's room and wait for him to come to me." She moved lithely toward the door, then paused to add, "I really wouldn't expect us for dinner. We're planning on being very occupied."

The door closed behind her with a definite click, and Sheena made a sound somewhere between a moan of pain and a growl of rage. Rushing to the window seat, she snatched up a tartan cushion and threw it at the closed door. Then she turned and threw herself on the bed, her fists beating the pillows in a furious tattoo. She had never felt so positively savage as when she had stood confronting that sweet, smiling witch. It would have taken just one more word to sweep aside her last inhibitions and provoke her to physically attack the model like a cave woman protecting her mate. The picture that her last words had evoked had nearly sent her berserk. How dare that woman think she could just crawl into Rand's bed and resume where they had left off four months ago! Rand Challon was hers, damn it! There was no way she was going to let that sex-crazed slut within a mile of him.

She jumped up from the bed and dressed quickly, then tore out of the room and down the stairs. She marched down the hall and was about to knock stridently on the closed study door when Laura Bradford came out of the kitchen and leaned against the doorjamb, her brandy-colored eyes appraising Sheena's distraught appearance thoughtfully.

"I wouldn't go in there right now," the older woman said quietly. "He's with Dr. Knowleton, and he said he didn't want to be disturbed." She smiled wryly. "If you're going to have a rhubarb, it's always best to do it in privacy. Why don't you come in and have a cup of coffee with me? It will give you a chance to get your thoughts together before you light into the boy. I can assure you that you're probably going to need it. He's tough as rawhide, and he learned his battle tactics in the corporate boardroom."

Sheena's hand slowly fell to her side, and she turned away from the closed door. Laura was right. She wanted no witnesses to her confrontation with Challon. She could wait until he was through with Knowleton. In all truth, she had no idea what she was going to say to Rand. She had been driven by a wild anger and jealousy that had completely banished logic from her mental processes. She had been so confused by the sudden riot of emotions that had been generated by Donna Scott that her only conscious thought had been to run to him and find some way of keeping him from going to his mistress.

She shook her head as if to clear it. What had she been thinking? She had no claim to Challon, nor did she wish to have. No, that was not true. She had felt such a fierce, primitive possessiveness at the thought of Rand in bed with that beautiful slut that they might have been married for a dozen years. Why should she feel like that if she wasn't emotionally involved with the man?

She ran a hand distractedly through her dark tangle of curls. "Yes, perhaps you're right." She turned to walk slowly toward the waiting Laura Bradford. "I don't seem to be thinking any too clearly at the moment."

Laura Bradford gave her a surprisingly gentle smile. "It goes with the territory, I understand," she said, turning and preceding Sheena back into the kitchen. "You're entitled, after what Rand put you through this morning."

Laura took two cups and saucers from the cabinet and grabbed the glass pot of coffee from the heating element of the coffeemaker. "Go sit down by the fire," she ordered briskly, shaking her head as Sheena offered to take the cups from her. "I wouldn't trust you to carry a feather pillow in the state you're in."

Sheena obediently sat down at the maple dining table in front of the fire. Laura Bradford sat down across from her and silently poured the coffee, then leaned forward to study Sheena's face in the firelight. "You're as wild-eyed and nervous as a newborn colt," she said gruffly. "I don't think Rand imagined that his playacting was going to upset you this much." Her brandy brown eyes narrowed consideringly. "Or maybe he did. He might have thought shaking you up a little might be to his advantage."

"Playacting?" Sheena asked bitterly. "I think you're mistaken, Laura. There was no reason for Rand to be anything but perfectly frank with me. He owes me nothing but my freedom." She looked down blindly at the coffee in her cup. "It's clear that he's merely realized that he's made a mistake where I'm concerned. Miss Scott has apparently managed to stir up the embers of their affair to quite a respectable blaze in an amazingly short time."

Laura Bradford snorted derisively. "Don't be stupid. Rand doesn't give a damn about Donna Scott. He's a man, and she was available. He's a very virile man, for God's sake. There have been more woman than I can count in Rand's bed over the years, and Donna Scott doesn't mean any more than the rest of them. After a month he can barely recall their names."

"I imagine he finds their anatomies a trifle more memorable," Sheena said tartly, stung by the thought of that parade of faceless women.

"Perhaps." Laura Bradford chuckled, her brown eyes twinkling. "But to my knowledge, he's never kept a photo of any one of them to remind him."

"Some people collect stamps. Rand collects pictures of Irish folksingers." Sheena's dark eyes turned stormy once again. "I was foolish to believe him when he said they meant something special to him. Probably next year he'll have a roomful of photos of that blond bombshell upstairs."

"You're wrong," the older woman said. "But I can see that Rand has you wound up so tight that you can't see straight." She took a sip of coffee and sat back, her plain, freckled face serene. "Well, perhaps it's better if you thrash it out with him. It's obviously what he wants, and it might clear the air."

"Why should I give him anything that he wants? It seems to me that Rand Challon has had his own way entirely too much in our relationship. Perhaps it's time I made a few decisions." She pushed away the coffee cup.

"For instance?" Laura Bradford asked, her eyes on the mutinous curve of Sheena's lips.

"It appears that this little hideaway is getting a bit crowded," Sheena said. "I think it's time I moved on and let Donna Scott have her turn at your irresistible charge. I'm sure that she'd be more than happy to arrange my departure."

"Don't do it, Sheena. Rand very seldom loses his temper, but you wouldn't want to be around when he does."

Sheena looked up, poignant pain mixed with the defiance in her dark eyes. "Why should he be angry? He'll probably be grateful to me for removing an awkward obstacle in his path. I've heard there's nothing so cold as the ashes of a dead love affair." Her lips twisted. "And in our case, there isn't even that to regret. Yes, I think I'll have a little talk with Miss Scott later tonight." She pushed back her chair and stood up.

"I don't suppose you'll believe me if I tell you that you're making a serious mistake?" Laura asked. Then as Sheena shook her head stubbornly, Laura gave a resigned sigh. "I didn't think so. I should have saved my breath." She watched with troubled eyes as Sheena strode belligerently toward the door. "Where are you going?"

"I'm going out for a long walk," Sheena said over her shoulder, her dark eyes feverishly restless in her white face. "Don't wait dinner for me, Laura." Her lips curved in a bitter smile. "You needn't make my excuses to Rand. His mistress assured me that they'd be too busy for dinner tonight."

Six

It was almost dark when Sheena made her reluctant way back to the cabin through the dense forest. She had put off her return as long as possible, but when twilight covered the pine forest with its frigid blanket, she knew it would be foolish to delay any longer. It would be very easy to lose her way when darkness obscured the landmarks she had become familiar with in her walks with Challon. All she needed was to have Rand forced to call out a search party to find her. He would find it most inconvenient if he had to interrupt his rendezvous with that luscious blond amazon, she thought gloomily.

Sheena pushed that distasteful thought away hurriedly as she had all similar ones on her lone tramp through the woods. It seemed that she had walked endlessly, setting a brisk pace in the hope that the activity would help to keep her from thinking. She had purposely avoided the fallen pine tree at the head of the lake, for she knew it would bring back far too many memories. They had made a habit of stopping to rest there after that first day. Rand would scoop her up and settle her in his lap and they would talk lazily and contentedly until Sheena was recovered enough to resume their walk. Now that memory was as agonizing as the hundreds of others that they had shared. How could so few days build so many memories? she wondered miserably.

"So you finally decided to come back." Rand's voice whipped through the still forest like the crack of a lariat.

She stopped abruptly in the center of the path, her eyes widening in surprise. She had almost reached the edge of the forest, and Challon was standing in the path before her, looming ominously large in the quickly darkening woods. She could not see his features, but there was a tightly coiled tension in his stance that sent a shiver of fear through her.

"You needn't have come to find me," Sheena said, glaring at him defiantly. "I know these woods fairly well now, and I was quite safe. There was no reason for you to have left Miss Scott."

Challon swore under his breath. "Sheena, if you say one more word, I won't wait until I get you back to the cabin to teach you a lesson you won't forget!" He had reached her now, and his hand clamped onto her wrist with steely strength. "I don't think you'd find a bed of pine needles in zero weather even a little bit titillating." He was pulling her swiftly after him, and she had to trot to keep up. "While I probably wouldn't even know the difference. You've got me so damn hot, both mentally *and* physically, that I'd probably burn the woods down!"

"You're not making sense," she protested breathlessly, as he pulled her up the hill toward the cabin. "And I don't appreciate your acting like some macho caveman just because I interrupted your tête à tête with Miss Scott." She struggled vainly to release her wrist. "It's not my fault that you decided to come after me. I told Laura that I didn't want any dinner."

"That's good," he said grimly. "Because I doubt if either one of us will get anything to eat tonight. I plan on keeping you very busy."

They had reached the sundeck now, and Sheena noticed bewilderedly that the cabin was strangely dim and deserted looking. Darkness had fallen now, and Challon opened the door and pushed her inside, flicking on the light as he did so.

"Where is everybody?" Sheena asked, confused.

"Gone," He pulled her toward the fireplace, where a blaze was burning fitfully. Shrugging out of his sheepskin jacket, he tossed it carelessly on the beige couch, then turned to unbutton her coat.

"Gone where?" Sheena asked blankly, as he pushed the coat down her arms and then threw it beside his own on the couch.

"Houston," he said succinctly. He rubbed her cold hands briskly between his own. "You're half frozen. You'll be lucky if you don't end up back in your sickbed. Sit down, and I'll get you a brandy." He moved swiftly across the room to the small portable bar in the corner.

"Houston!" Sheena echoed blankly. "But why? I thought the plan was for them to leave later tonight. And why did Laura leave? She wasn't planning on going with them at all."

"She changed her mind." Challon returned to stand before her, the brandy glass in his hand. "Or perhaps I should say that I changed it for her. I decided that I'd had enough of chaperons to last me a lifetime. It was time we got back to a one-to-one basis as I planned originally."

Sheena ignored the brandy he held out to her and moved to stand before the fire, her hands outstretched to the flames. "May I ask where your gorgeous Miss Scott has gone? Have you arranged another little hideaway to stash her in? You're going to be a very busy man, aren't you?"

He followed her to the fireplace and put the brandy glass to her lips. "Drink this!" he ordered harshly. "I'm in no mood to listen to that asp's tongue without retaliation. So I'd advise you just to keep still."

She was forced to drink the brandy or have it dribble ignominiously down her chin as he tilted the glass. The brandy was hot going down, and she realized grudgingly that she had been chilled. However, the acknowledgment didn't lessen the resentment she was feeling.

"Satisfied?" she asked defiantly, as he took the empty glass away from her lips.

"Not by a long shot," he said. "But it's the tip of the iceberg. You just might get there yet." He put the glass down on the coffee table before the couch. Then he took her hand and began pulling her across the living room toward the staircase. "Let's go to bed."

She struggled futilely to free her arm as she stumbled after him. Her temper was rising with every step. "Will you let me go! Your mistress may like this sort of treatment, but I find it as revolting as I do you. I'm not some type of chattel for you to order about at will."

"For your information, Donna hasn't been my mistress for almost four months." Challon started up the stairs dragging her behind him. "But you might well wish that she had been before the night's over. I haven't touched another woman since I went to your first concert in Houston, and I'm damn near wild."

"I could see that at brunch when you told your mistress to go to your bedroom," Sheena said tartly, her dark eyes flashing. "I hope she proved satisfactory."

They had reached the top of the staircase, and he turned to face her, his golden eyes blazing. He reached out and shook her with no pretense of gentleness. "You've got to be the most obtuse bitch it's ever been my misfortune to know," he rasped hoarsely, his lean face taut with anger. "I'd just spent two of the most bloody, frustrating weeks of my life acting the gentle, considerate lover, so that you could see that you meant more to me than a romp in the hay. Does it make any sense that I'd give up all the gains I'd made, just to tumble a woman I don't give a damn about?"

Sheena was a trifle intimidated by the raw fury in Challon's face, but she was careful not to show it. "Well, it was very clear that was exactly what you had in mind," she said belligerently. "You treated me like a little sister from the minute she stepped off the plane, and you told her that—"

"I know what I told her," he interrupted. "I had to tell her that, damn it! No one was supposed to know you were here. Donna would have spread the juicy tidbit that I had you tucked away up here all over Houston. O'Shea is bound to be doing some snooping around. Your sudden disappearance and my arrival on the scene was too pat a coincidence to escape scrutiny."

"So you decided to take her to bed to keep her mouth shut," Sheena scoffed, her black eyes flashing. "I'm not entirely the fool, Rand Challon!"

"The hell you're not. I know how to handle Donna, and it wouldn't have gone that far, damn it. All you had to do was to keep a low profile, and everything would have been fine. Donna would have been on that plane tonight purring like a kitten, her lips firmly sealed."

"I believe that she would have been purring, but I doubt if she'd have been on the plane!" Sheena said hotly.

"You jealous little shrew," Challon accused furiously, his golden eyes darkening to amber. "Don't you realize what you've done? After Laura told me what you planned on doing, I had to scratch everything and hustle everybody back on the jet for Houston. I didn't dare wait and give you a chance to blow everything sky-high."

"I'm not jealous! You have to care about someone to be jealous, and I couldn't care less about you or your sexy models!" She tilted her chin defiantly. "Do you hear me, Rand Challon? I care nothing at all for you."

He shook her again, this time much harder than before. "You're lying! You do love me, damn it. You're just too stubborn to admit it. You're scared out of your wits everyone will realize that you're a live, flesh-and-blood woman and not just a sacrifice on your brother's funeral pyre." His face was granite hard as he continued tersely. "Well, I'm tired of waiting for you to say the words. You're mine, and we both know it."

He ignored her cry of indignant rage as he scooped her up in his arms and carried her kicking and struggling to her bedroom. After manipulating the doorknob with some difficulty, he entered and kicked the door shut behind him. He put her down just inside the door, and turning the key in the lock, he removed it and stuffed it carelessly in his pocket. The room was dark, but instead of flicking on the light, he moved with the lithe sureness of a cat to the fireplace and knelt to light the logs.

Sheena whirled and pulled and rattled at the knob futilely, before turning to face Challon. "I'll fight you," she told him fiercely. "You'll have to rape me."

"No, I won't." The logs caught fire and flamed up, suddenly lighting the rugged, lean planes of his face. He rose slowly to his feet and came toward her with the easy grace of a man who had all the time in the world. "It will be exactly as it would have been if I hadn't decided to act like a quixotic ass of a Galahad."

He had reached her now and picked her up with easy strength and carried her to the chaise longue in front of the fire, subduing her struggles as if they didn't exist. He set her down and stepped back to look at her. "It will be the same as it's always going to be for us, Sheena." His hands were unfastening the buttons of his brown suede shirt, and as he stripped it off and threw it aside he said, "It's going to be the best damn thing that's ever happened to either of us."

The glow of the fire illuminated the brawny, powerful muscles of his hair-roughened chest, and Sheena caught her breath at the sheer, savage beauty of him. The reflection of the fire was in the clear gold blaze of his eyes, and the sun-bleached streaks in his crisp, tawny mane suddenly came vibrantly alive. He was all power, muscle, and aggressive, driving male as he stood there. The golden man, she thought dazedly, feeling that familiar liquid melting as she looked at him.

"Don't do this, Rand," she pleaded faintly, as he knelt before her, his hands busy on the buttons of her shirt. "I don't want this to happen."

"You will." He pushed the blouse aside and deftly unfastened her bra. "We don't have a choice now."

"There's always a choice," she said huskily. Her anger had inexplicably vanished as she sat almost meekly and watched him as he pushed the blouse and bra down over her arms. It was crazy, but she was suddenly experiencing that same sense of rightness, that ephemeral feeling of homecoming that she had felt that day in the woods.

He went abruptly still and inhaled sharply as his eyes fixed on her small, perfect breasts, their pink rosettes blooming tautly in the flickering firelight. "God, you're so damn lovely," he said huskily, his hands reaching out to cup her breasts in his hands. The hard ruthlessness had vanished from his face as all resistance had fled from hers. "Don't fight me, sweetheart. The *last* thing I want in the world is to hurt you." He drew her carefully forward as if she were infinitely fragile, and she flowed toward him as irresistibly as the tide to the shore.

A great shudder shook his body as her bare breasts brushed against his chest, which was moving spasmodically with the force of his ragged breathing. "God, little dove, I didn't want it to be like this," he murmured thickly. "But I can't risk your leaving me as you nearly did tonight. You've got to know that we belong to each other in all the ways there are. Don't hate me, love."

There was almost a note of pleading in that arrogant voice, and it touched her with a poignancy that caused her throat to tighten with unshed tears. How completely daft it was to feel this surge of maternal tenderness, when her nipples were burning from the abrasive contact with his tawny pelt and her bones felt as if they'd melted away entirely.

His hands were drawing teasing patterns on her supple back, and his lips were brushing gently at her ear. "Just relax, dove. I promise that there will be nothing but pleasure for you tonight in my arms. I never want you to know anything but pleasure, ever again."

Sheena could feel the rapid throbbing of his heart against her own, and it had the mesmeric effect of a metronome, while the evocative words both aroused and, conversely, soothed her. Then his hands were at the fastener at the waistband of her jeans. She knew that she should stop him, but somehow she couldn't remember why. His hands were so deft and certain. The expression on his face was so tender and sure, that it all seemed the most supremely natural thing in the world to let him strip her of her jeans and the tiny satin bikini panties beneath.

Then, his bronze face beautifully intense, he threw the garments aside and with gentle, careful hands moved her up on the chaise longue so that she was half sitting, half reclining. Sheena knew no shyness or embarrassment as he sat down beside her and merely sat looking at her for a long rapt moment as she lay before him in the light of the flickering flames. Instead, there was a fierce, primitive pride racing through her at the knowledge that the sight of her could bring that look of taut hunger and passionate intentness to his face.

"This is another one of my fantasies," he said raggedly, his golden gaze running over her with a loving intimacy. "But the reality is much more exciting than my imaginings. There's only one thing missing."

His head bent slowly to her breast, and his tongue began a teasing arousal of the nipple, which caused a hot shudder of need to ripple through her. Rand must have felt the eager response of her body, for a low, pleased laugh broke from him. His teeth joined in the playful torment, and the gentle nibbling at the already engorged nipples caused her suddenly to clutch at his shoulders to bring him closer.

He raised his head, and then his lips were on hers in a branding, passionate kiss, his tongue plunging into her mouth to search out and joust erotically with her own. They were both breathless when he pushed her gently from him and raised his head once again to look at her. His golden eyes had darkened to amber as his gaze traveled over her swollen breasts, their pink tips taut and aroused, then moved up to her face, which was dreamy and languid with desire.

"Now the fantasy is complete," he said huskily. "I knew your face would have just that look of passionate gypsy abandonment." His hand was slightly shaky as he placed it on her silken belly and rubbed the soft skin sensuously. "But the rest of you is so tiny and delicate. You're like a lovely, perfectly formed child. I never noticed that you had that almost breakable quality."

"Rand." Sheena's voice was throaty with need as his warm hands traveled caressingly down to her thighs, his eyes fixed in fascination on the flesh his hands were kneading and fondling. "I want—"

He leaned forward swiftly and interrupted her with a hard, passionate kiss. "God, Sheena, I can't stop now." He groaned. "I can't help it if you want me to let you go." His hands were moving over her feverishly, kneading and caressing her body, which was already aroused to an exquisite sensitivity, and she gave a low moan that was almost animallike.

Sheena had no intention of asking him to cease this fiery torment of the senses. Indeed, she didn't know if she could have mustered the strength to stop him if she had been as reluctant as Rand believed. She was immersed in a whirlpool of sensation. She was vividly aware of her body and each electric response that Rand's hands and lips was wresting from it. The liquid throbbing ache in her loins was almost unbearable, but she had no desire to end it. What had Rand said about the exquisite pain of anticipation? she thought hazily.

But it seemed that Rand had reached the end of his patience, for he was scooping her up in his arms and carrying her to the four-poster bed across the room. As he laid her down on the red tartan spread, he stepped back, and his hands worked with deft speed at his belt.

It seemed only seconds before he joined her on the bed and gathered her with swift urgency to his hard arousal. She was vividly conscious of the sleek male beauty of his powerful shoulders, lean, tapering waist, and tight, muscular buttocks, all of which were bathed in a flickering patina of gold.

He looked down at her, his eyes curiously searching. "I can't wait any longer, dove," he said hoarsely. "Tell me that you know why I'm doing this. Tell me that you understand."

Sheena met that pleading look with a tranquil serenity in her dark eyes. "I understand," she whispered.

She did understand, and far more than he was asking of her. Suddenly all the pieces had flowed together, and all confusion and turmoil had vanished as if they had never existed. She knew with rocklike certainty that she loved this man. Why hadn't she realized it this morning when she had been so torn apart with hurt and jealousy that she had become physically ill? Now it appeared the most logical thing in the world that she should love Rand Challon. He was right, she had come home.

Then one hair-roughened thigh parted her own, and she forgot about everything but the dizzying excitement of hard hands and deft fingers that probed with rhythmic urgency until she was moaning and writhing beneath Rand like a woman demented. When he moved forward between her thighs to broach the final barrier, she surged toward him with such passionate eagerness that he gave a laugh of sheer delight.

When he was finally sheathed in her warmth, he looked down at her with an expression of almost pained pleasure. "Oh, God, you feel so good," he gasped. His hips started to plunge with wild urgency. "You're driving me out of my mind, love."

She found she couldn't answer with anything but keening little mating croons, which were eminently satisfying to the man above her. "That's right, sing for me, little lark," he whispered, as his hands closed on her hips and lifted her to meet his gyrating thighs. "Let me hear you moan with pleasure, love."

He was not disappointed as the wild, spiraling tension mounted to breathless peaks of ecstasy. Sheena could feel the tears running helplessly down her face as he brought her to the edge of that final mind-jolting moment only to hold her back at the last instant. It wasn't until her body was moving as wildly and demandingly as his own in a desperate effort to attain that ultimate glory that he at last took her with him in an erotic star-spangled explosion that left them both panting and clinging to each other like two shipwrecked souls.

Sheena was still crushed in Challon's arms a few moments later when he rolled over on his side, taking her with him. He lifted his head to stare down at her in lazy contentment. "Stay with me, sweetheart," he said softly. "God, you feel sweet around me."

Sheena nestled her head in the hollow of his shoulder. She had no desire to move even the tiniest muscle, she thought with a drowsy euphoria. She had an odd sensation that more than their bodies had been linked in that white-hot merging. It was as if there were a cord now stretched between them binding her mental and emotional responses to Rand's. She gave a sigh that was more like a contented purr.

Rand kissed her delicate, blue-veined temple. "Lord, I must have been insane to wait so long," he said huskily. "Do you realize that what we've just had is one in a million?"

Sheena's chuckle was laced with mischief as she said

lightly, "Really? That's too bad. I was hoping it would be just as good the second time."

"Brat." Rand tangled his hand in her curls and tilted her head back to kiss her lightly. "Didn't anyone ever tell you that a moment like this is no time to exercise that puckish Irish humor? Don't you realize that this is a very solemn moment, woman? You've just yielded that nubile body and the prize of your virginity to my insatiable lust."

"I really didn't notice," she said airily. "You must have done it very well." She looked up at him, her dark eyes dancing. "As for your insatiable lust, it appears to me that you're more than replete."

"Only temporarily." He growled, pressing her head back into his shoulder. "Even we insatiable satyrs have to take a break."

Sheena gave a throaty giggle. "I'm glad you explained that. I wouldn't want to think that I'd completely sapped your strength."

"Sapped!" Rand yelped indignantly, one admonitory hand giving her pert derriere a sharp slap. "We'll see who is 'sapped' by morning, my fine colleen. You won't be able to get out of bed for a week. I can see right now that I'm going to have to start bending the twig in the way the tree should grow, or you're going to prove a perfect shrew of a wife."

Sheena went suddenly still. "Wife?" she asked faintly.

Somehow she hadn't thought past that first ecstatic realization of her love for Rand. The sudden self-acknowledgment of her feelings followed immediately by the lovemaking that had shaken her to her foundations had blocked all possible repercussions of her actions from her mind.

"Wife," Challon asserted firmly. "We'll fly to Las Vegas tomorrow to be married."

Sheena made a tiny movement of instinctive withdrawal, which was immediately thwarted by Rand's possessive arms. She shook her head bewilderedly. "You're going too fast," she protested. "I can't just run off and get married without proper thought." She rolled away from the warm nearness of his body, and this time he let her go.

Rand's eyes were narrowed, the lazy contentment wiped entirely from his face. "What's to think about?" he asked curtly. "I want you, and I know damn well you want me. You can't deny now that you know I can make you happy." His lips twisted bitterly. "Even if I have to keep you in bed twenty-four hours a day to accomplish it."

Sheena sat up, wrapping the tartan spread around her and tucking the material beneath her arms. She ran her hand through her cloud of gypsy curls. "But I have responsibilities," she said, biting her lip worriedly. "I have a career and Uncle Donal to think about. I can't just abandon everything we've worked for with no notice, whatever." She turned her troubled gaze on him. "I'll have to give him time to adjust to the idea. Give me six months or a year to fulfill my commitments and let me gradually ease him into it."

"No way," Challon said harshly, and sat upright. "I'm not letting you go back to O'Shea. I'll buy you the best showcase in the business if you want to continue your career, but I won't let that bastard crucify you again."

"You don't understand," she protested helplessly, fixing her eyes pleadingly on his lean, rugged face, which had taken on an expression of implacable ruthlessness.

"No, you're the one who doesn't understand," he retorted, his golden eyes flaming. "You can marry me tomorrow and let me love you and care for you for the rest of your life, or we'll keep on with the status quo. There's no other choice."

"But you can't mean to still keep me prisoner," Sheena said incredulously. It had never occurred to her that he could possibly expect to resume their former roles of captor and prisoner after all that had passed between them tonight.

"You're damn right I can. Maybe you don't love me, but we've got a hell of a good basis for a marriage, and you know it." His lips tightened. "There's no possibility of my releasing you to go back to the life you were leading, so you can just make up your mind to either give in or be my 'guest' until you're a little, white-haired old lady."

Not love him? Sheena bit her lip painfully to keep back the words of love that wanted to tumble out in reckless abandonment. The temptation to surrender to his demands was almost irresistible. In that moment the thought of belonging to him in the total commitment of marriage seemed the most desirable thing she had ever known. For that very reason, she knew that she must not tell him how much he meant to her. If he realized how she felt about him, he would move with relentless efficiency to vanquish her every objection, no matter how valid.

"I think we both know that you can't keep me here indefinitely," she said quietly, not looking at him. "I've told you that I have obligations that must be met. Why can't you just let me go?"

"No!" the answer came with almost menacing ruthlessness. "I may not be able to keep you forever, but it will be long enough. You're not experienced enough to know that sexual encounters like the one we had tonight can be quite addictive. Give me another month with you, and you won't be able to do without your fix."

"And what if I refuse to submit to your lovemaking?" Sheena asked coolly. "You can hardly develop a habit if you don't indulge."

His lips twisted cynically. "I don't think I need worry about that. You're a very passionate lady, Sheena." One lazy hand reached out to caress her breast through the cover, and her nipple hardened in response. Rand mockingly arched one sandy brow. "You see?" he asked softly. "You're ready for me again, aren't you, dove?"

"No," she protested, moistening her lips nervously.

"Yes," he said, pulling her with hard sureness back into his arms. "And I'm ready for you." With one swift movement, he stripped the spread away from her nude body. His face took on a glazed absorption as he looked down at her. "I'll always be ready for you."

He bent his head slowly and kissed her with a hot, lingering sweetness. It was only an instant later that her arms slid slowly over his shoulders and around his neck to pull him closer to her with the same desperate urgency that she sensed in him. She knew that she would always be ready for him, too.

"Come on, sleepyhead, you look entirely too enticing lying there. If you don't get up, I'm going to crawl back in bed with you, and we don't have time for what would follow."

Sheena lifted heavy lids to stare, with drowsy contentment, at Rand's amused face. He looked so beautiful, she thought sleepily, reaching out a hand to stroke the tawny pelt of hair on his bronze chest. It was slightly damp, and she vaguely realized that he was just out of the shower. He had only a white towel wrapped around his hips as he sat on the side of the bed, and his sun-bleached hair was darkened by the wetting to a shade close to its original tan.

Her caressing hand was caught firmly by his and raised to his lips for a lingering kiss. "And none of your beguiling little tricks, dove. I won't be seduced this morning, no matter what the temptation. We have to get moving."

"You called me lark last night," Sheena said dreamily, hearing only the first sentence. Despite the mock sternness of his expression, she had little doubt that she could persuade Rand to change his mind once she could bestir herself to make the effort. No persuasion was really necessary on either side, she thought. They were as combustible together as a runaway forest fire. She couldn't remember how many times they had come together during the night in the passionate fusion that had been just as world-shaking as that first time. Rand had uncovered depths of sensuality in her that she had never known existed. She found herself not only responding but aggressively initiating their loveplay until sheer exhaustion caused them to fall asleep in each other's arms like two weary children.

"Last night you were a lark," Rand said softly, his gaze running tenderly over her swollen pink lips and the radiant bloom on her cheeks. "You spread your golden wings and took off right for the sun."

"Yet this morning I'm delegated back to the rank of dove," she said lightly.

There was an odd flicker in the depths of Rand's eyes, and his lips tightened. "You've got to earn your wings, Sheena. Nothing comes free in this world, not even the knowledge of self. You can't remain wrapped in a protective cocoon all your life. You've got to come out in the real world with the rest of us."

"You're suddenly very serious," she said nervously, not looking at him. There was a ruthlessness in his words that had abruptly shattered her sense of well-being. "I thought I had dealt with a greater amount of unpleasant reality than most people."

He shook his head. "You didn't deal with it. You experienced it, and then you ran to your uncle like a child afraid of the dark and let him tell you what you should be feeling." Wearily he ran his hand through his tawny hair. "The hell of it was that you *were* only a child at the time. How could anyone expect you to do anything else?"

Sheena slowly sat up and tucked the sheet around her. "I suppose I should be grateful for your understanding," she said caustically. "It's easy to stand back and be objective if you're not involved. It's a bit different if it's happening to you."

Rand's expression softened as his hand stroked her tousled curls. "I know, little dove. I'm probably being a bit of a bastard to you. It's just that I get so damned impatient. I don't suppose you've changed your mind about marrying me?"

Sheena shook her head stubbornly. "Don't you see

that it's not possible right now?" she asked, her dark eyes bright with tears. "Would it be so unreasonable to give me the time I ask of you?"

Rand's expression was serious. "More unreasonable than you know, dove," he said quietly. "So it seems that we're back to square one."

"You haven't changed your mind, either," Sheena said. It was a statement, not a question. She had known the night before that Rand's iron determination would not be shaken by any arguments she could muster.

"Why should I?" Rand asked mockingly. "The second stage of your captivity promises to be even more exciting than the first. Who knows? Now that some of my frustrations have been pacified, we may even reach a more harmonious mental rapport as well." His hand moved from her hair to strike her cheek with an almost sensuous enjoyment. "Besides, I've only begun getting you hooked on the world's greatest sport. You're going to need quite a few more injections before I'll be satisfied that you're a full-fledged addict." He gave her a quick, hard kiss, then rose reluctantly to his feet. "Now, move woman! We're running late already."

"Late?" Sheena asked bewilderedly, her eyes going to the clock on the bedside table. "It's barely eight o'clock. Why are we running late?"

"We're closing up the cabin and flying out of here in approximately forty-five minutes," he said briskly. "While you shower, I'll finish dressing and turn off the generator. John should have the jet on the approach right now."

Sheena clutched at the sheet, her eyes widening with surprise. "But where are we going?" she asked. "And why are we in such a hurry?"

"We're going home," he said simply. Then his lips twisted wryly. "Well, almost home. I can't take you to Crescent Creek while you're still a nominal prisoner, so we'll be going to an adjoining property that I've recently acquired. It's quite a nice little ranch. We'll be very cozy there." He was walking toward the door as he continued, "I was actually planning on taking you away from here, anyway. Knowleton told me yesterday that I should get you to a warmer climate so that you could rid yourself of that nagging little cough. You just accelerated things a bit by causing me to throw Donna out of here without assuring her silence. This isn't a safe place for you now; we'll have to leave at once. I told John yesterday before he took off that he was to return this morning to pick us up."

He turned at the door, his golden eyes lit with sudden mischief. "If you're a very good girl and don't keep me waiting, I just may let you persuade me to initiate you into the mile-high club that I mentioned."

He closed the door softly behind him, leaving her to stare after him in befuddled amazement.

Seven

The wave of dry heat struck Sheena like a blow as the door of the jet was opened and the steps were lowered at the private landing strip at Crescent Creek. From the air, the runway and hangar had looked as if they had been dropped in the middle of nowhere, and when she had commented on the fact to Rand, he had explained that his private airport was located some twenty-five miles from the main residence and outbuildings.

"I leave a few security men and mechanics on duty at all times," he had added. "But I've found that isolating the strip is the only way to maintain the degree of privacy that I require at the ranch." He smiled grimly. "It's my own early warning system."

Since she was aware of the seclusion of the strip, it came as no surprise to see a sturdy Renegade jeep parked at the edge of the tarmac a short distance away. But the driver of the vehicle obviously awaiting their arrival was another matter entirely. The young man leaning indolently against the fender of the canary yellow jeep straightened slowly as Rand swung her down from the steps and they started across the tarmac.

"Great heavens!" Sheena said, startled. "Can the man be real?"

"Oh, he's real all right," Challon replied. "I think Nick must have seen a John Wayne movie when he was a kid, and he's been afraid of disappointing the lady tourists with less than the real thing ever since. I didn't realize that he'd be the one to meet us, or I would have warned you about Nick O'Brien. He takes a little getting used to." In spite of the ambiguous words, there was a note of warm affection in Challon's voice that caused Sheena to look with even greater interest at the colorful figure by the jeep.

Nick O'Brien was an incredibly handsome man in his twenties of obvious Latin extraction. His gleaming dark hair was worn a trifle long and trendily styled. His features had the aristocratic definity of a modern-day Montezuma, and his eyes were a startling aquamarine that fairly crackled with vitality and good spirits.

It was not his dazzling good looks that amazed her so much as his outfit. A stunning red shirt was teamed with a black leather vest for the maximum dramatic effect. And his black jeans were surely the tightest she had ever seen. The denim material molded his powerful thighs and calves with a detailed closeness that was almost indecent. His black boots were polished to a mirrorlike shine, and glittering silver spurs complimented the silver Indian belt encircling his narrow waist.

"He's quite—unusual," Sheena said faintly, her eyes fixed in fascination on O'Brien's arresting figure. "O'Brien? He doesn't look at all Irish."

"He's part Irish, part Mexican, and part pure devil. So don't think you've found a soulmate in Nick, no matter how charming you may find him. He's as dangerous as a high explosive."

"Yet you're very fond of him," Sheena said thoughtfully. "Does he work for you?"

"When he's in the mood," Rand answered, shrugging. "I never know when he's going to show up. His father is chairman of the board of O'Brien Computers, and Nick is rich as Croesus in his own right. When it amuses him to play cowboy, he pays me a little visit. Then, when boredom sets in, he's gone like a will-o'-the-wisp."

"He's something of a playboy then?" Sheena asked. He certainly looked the role, and she was certain those virile good looks must be magnetically attractive to the opposite sex.

"Because of his low boredom threshhold?" Challon shook his head. "It's not that simple, I'm afraid. How old do you think Nick is?"

"He looks to be about twenty-five," Sheena estimated, wondering what on earth that had to do with anything.

"He's twenty-four. And it may interest you to know that he has a doctorate in both electrical engineering and computer sciences, and can speak and write seven languages.

"But that's impossible!"

"I'm glad you realize that," Rand drawled, his golden eyes twinkling. "It will better enable you to understand him. Nick *is* impossible. He's a genius on the same scale as Einstein. Besides having an IQ that runs right off the scale, he has a photographic memory that permits perfect recall. Do you wonder that he gets bored and restless fairly easily?"

"No, I guess not. I always thought geniuses were pale little men with stooped shoulders and horn-rimmed glasses."

"Nick's degree of intelligence together with determination allows him to do pretty near anything well. I first ran into Nick in a dive in Algiers three years ago. I was having a spot of trouble with an Arab guide and his friends, who wanted to liberate me from my wallet. Nick joined in the free-for-all, and let me tell you, I was damn glad to have him at my back. He's as good at barroom brawling as he is at developing new computer languages."

They had almost reached the jeep, and O'Brien stepped forward, his smile flashing brilliantly in his tanned face. "Howdy, boss," he drawled, sticking out his hand in greeting to Challon. "Welcome back to the old homestead."

Rand shook his hand before saying dryly, "You can cut the Randolph Scott bit, Nick. I've already tipped your hand to Sheena. What are you doing here, anyway? The last I heard, you were in Las Vegas working out a formula to break the system. Did you finally meet your Waterloo?"

O'Brien grinned. "Nope. It took a bit of research, but I finally found the key. After that it was all downhill. Unfortunately, a large delegation of the casino owners weren't exactly happy with my accomplishment. I was requested most forcefully to leave."

Rand shook his head ruefully. "You're lucky you didn't get killed. Don't you ever get tired of taking chances?"

O'Brien shrugged carelessly. "It's one way of knowing you're alive." His flashing aquamarine eyes were suddenly dancing. "It's just as well that I decided not to make a stand. When I arrived at Crescent Creek, it was only to find that my old buddy had taken off for parts unknown. I'd have been in a hell of a mess if I'd relied on you to back me this time. As it was, I've been bored as the devil waiting for you to get back."

"I rather imagine you've kept yourself busy," Rand said dryly. "How many hands has my foreman put on the sick list this time because of that damned restlessness?"

"Only a few," O'Brien said absently, his eyes now on Sheena. She felt suddenly uncomfortably naked as she met that piercing gaze. It turned out that she had reason for her uneasiness, for he said slowly, "Sheena Reardon, Ireland's Mournful Dove. Rand has pictures of you in his study."

Sheena sighed in exasperation. "It seems that everyone in the world must know about those photographs," she said crossly. "I should really hire the man as my publicist."

Rand's arm slid around her waist as he said soothingly, "It's not as bad as all that, dove. I guess I should have expected Nick to remember. He's never commented on them, so I really thought he hadn't noticed." He turned to the younger man. "I suppose that I'd better introduce you formally. Sheena Reardon, this imp of satan is Nick O'Brien, hired hand extraordinaire."

O'Brien bowed with a graceful panache, his grin flashing warmly. "I'm delighted to meet you, lovely lady. I can see now why Rand decided to become incommunicado if you were anywhere in the vicinity."

Sheena smiled at O'Brien's gallantry. She didn't feel in the least lovely in the jeans and rumpled red plaid shirt she was wearing, but he almost made her believe in his blarney. "Thank you. I'm very glad to meet you, too, Mr. O'Brien."

"Nick," he corrected, grinning. "You mustn't be too formal with the hired help. It makes us uppity."

"He's right," Rand said, grimacing. "Nick's arrogant enough without encouragement." Placing his hands on Sheena's waist, he lifted her up into the jeep. "Did Jesse get the Crawfords moved off the Triple X property?"

"All was done as you commanded, sire," O'Brien said mockingly. He climbed into the driver's seat and put the jeep in gear. Rand barely had time to jump into the seat beside Sheena before the vehicle took off like a bucking bronco over the rough, rutted road. Sheena instinctively grabbed Rand by the arm as the jeep sped over the ground at a dizzying pace. "Not that there wasn't a good deal of speculation at the ranch over your instructions," O'Brien shouted cheerfully, over the roar of the motor. "I even admit to a touch of curiosity as to the reason why you would move your manager and his wife out of their residence along with the entire crew and install them at Crescent Creek instead."

His aquamarine eyes shot them a flashing, sidelong glance. "It's a very interesting puzzle."

Rand's lips curved in a reluctant smile. "And you never could resist a puzzle, could you, Nick?" he asked.

"No, I never could," O'Brien replied, grinning mischievously. "My mental processes are inherently geared toward problem solving, but don't give me a hint, let me figure it out for myself."

"I fully intend to do just that," Rand said coolly, putting an arm possessively around Sheena's shoulders. "Enjoy yourself, Nick."

"I will," O'Brien assured him, as his booted foot gunned the accelerator to even greater speed. "I will."

It seemed mere minutes before the jeep left the stark, flat terrain behind and was traversing country that gradually took on a lush greenness. Though the country was nothing like the soft, misty fields of Ireland, it had a strong, serene beauty that Sheena found very pleasing.

The ranch house and outbuildings were equally pleasing, Sheena thought, as the jeep finally roared past the corral and came to a screeching stop before a small white clapboard house, whose roomy front porch sported a cozy, cushioned swing.

"Here we are," O'Brien announced. He shut off the engine and leaned both arms on the steering wheel. "I think I beat my last speed record on the way here by four minutes."

"I wouldn't doubt it," Rand said dryly, as he stepped down from the jeep and swung Sheena to the ground. "Remind me to fasten our seat belts next time."

"You're getting old, Rand," O'Brien scoffed. "I don't suppose you're going to invite me into the house for a drink?"

"That's right," Rand returned genially. "Why don't you get the hell out of here?"

"If you insist," O'Brien drawled. "I'll forgive you your churlishness as it's no doubt generated by your eagerness to be alone with that beautiful Irish colleen at your side." He winked at Sheena. "But you should try to conquer that rampant selfishness and let the rest of us poor males enjoy the sight of her. Did you know that there's a barn dance at the McAlisters' spread tonight?"

"No, and I can't say that it particularly interests me. We've had a long flight, and we're a little tired."

O'Brien's gaze moved to Sheena. "Your lovely guest doesn't look at all weary," he said softly, his voice coaxing. "Wouldn't you like to experience a piece of real Americana, O stranger to our shores?"

Rand's hand tightened warningly on her elbow, and Sheena suddenly felt a tinge of rebellion flood her. It was obvious that he didn't want her to mix with his friends and associates at the neighboring ranch. Perhaps he regarded it as a risk to his plans for her.

"I would indeed, Nick," she said, giving him a glowing smile. "How nice of you to think of it."

"Great!" O'Brien turned on the ignition. "I'll pick you both up at eight and chauffeur you over to the McAlisters' myself." Without waiting for a reply, he put the car into gear and tore off across the stable yard without even a backward glance at Challon's frowning face.

Rand muttered a very explicit obscenity beneath his breath and frowned at Sheena. "Perhaps I shouldn't have jumped to conclusions," he said grimly. "You and Nick may be soulmates at that. You both have a decided attraction for trouble. You knew damn well I didn't want to go to that party tonight."

"Yes, I did," Sheena said coolly. "It couldn't be because you were afraid that I'd find someone who would help me escape from you, could it?"

Rand shook his head as he propelled her up the porch steps. "Hell, no! I damn well own this particular part of the world. Everyone you'll meet tonight either owes me favors or would like to receive a few. The only thing you'd gain by making an appeal would be to embarrass both yourself and them." He opened the unlocked front door and allowed her to precede him into the small foyer. "I just wanted to avoid Nick as much as possible. When he gets an idea in his head, he worries it like a dog does a bone. I may end up having to tell him the whole story just to get him off my back."

"What a pity," Sheena said with dulcet sweetness. "Since he's evidently such a clever man, perhaps he'll realize just how criminally foolish this little adventure is."

"Don't count on any help from Nick, Sheena," Rand warned, his golden eyes narrowing menacingly. "He may be a wild devil, but he's a very loyal friend."

"We'll have to see about that," Sheena stated flippantly, then swept past him to the staircase to the left of the foyer. "Is my bedroom upstairs? I'd like to shower and change." She arched an eyebrow mockingly. "I suppose with your usual efficiency you've arranged for some clothes for me?"

"*Our* room is at the head of the stairs," Rand said grimly. "Our room, our bed, our life. Get used to it, dove. From now on we're a permanent team."

"Only if I choose it to be so," Sheena retorted, as she started up the stairs. "I'll not let you have it all your own way, Rand Challon." She looked back over her shoulder, her dark eyes challenging. "Well, do I have anything to wear tonight?"

There was a flicker of surprise mixed with what might have been admiration in his eyes. "You'll find everything you'll need in the closet in the master bedroom. I had some of your wardrobe transferred this afternoon from the guest room at Crescent Creek."

"I thought you might have," Sheena said coolly. "Is there a bathroom upstairs?"

Rand nodded. "Yes, milady," he drawled, watching her turn and climb the stairs with regal dignity. "Down the hall and to your left. I'll let you shower first, while I go to the kitchen and put on a pot of coffee. If you're determined to go out on the tiles tonight, we may need a dose of caffein. If you'll recall, we didn't get much sleep last night."

He gave a sudden amused chuckle as Sheena uttered an indignant exclamation. He then watched with an odd glint of pride in his eyes as she tilted her small nose in the air and disappeared up the stairs.

It was a wonderful party, Sheena thought hazily, as she moved slowly about the rough wooden floor in Rand's arms. She couldn't ever remember being to such a splendid occasion in all her life. The guests were splendid, the food was splendid, and the fruit punch was particularly splendid. Splendid was such a rich, meaningful word, and it exactly fitted her opinion of this wonderful evening, she thought dreamily. She nestled close to Rand's strong body, vaguely aware that some of the paper lanterns had been extinguished and that the huge barn had taken on a romantic atmosphere that was gloriously incongruous to the mundane surroundings. Glorious was a splendid word, too, she thought happily. She started humming softly along with the musicians, and she heard Rand's indulgent chuckle beneath her ear.

"How many trips did you make to the punch bowl this evening, dove?" he asked, as his arms tightened around her.

"What?" she asked vaguely, lifting her head to gaze into his golden eyes. What lovely eyes they were. They seemed to encompass all the laughter and tenderness in the world. "I don't remember. It was very good, though, wasn't it?"

"Very good." His voice was serious, but his eyes were twinkling. "And very potent. I should have kept a better eye on you, love. It's practically traditional for the boys to take turns spiking the punch."

"It had absolutely no effect on me, whatever," Sheena told him solemnly. "You see, I'm accustomed to good Irish whiskey."

"In staggering quantities, no doubt," Rand said, his lips twitching. "Have you ever heard of white lightning?"

"White lightning?" she asked, her dark eyes widening.

"Never mind, dove. I'll tell you all about it tomorrow. Did you have a good time at your first barn dance?"

"Oh, yes." she breathed enthusiastically. Slipping her arms about his waist, she nestled her head against his black cotton shirt. Rand was all in black, from his shiny black boots and jeans to the simple fitted western shirt that hugged his muscular shoulders with loving detail. The somber garments accentuated his tawny coloring. "I particularly liked the square dancing. It's a very vigorous folk dance, isn't it?"

"Very," he agreed. "Though you're such a featherweight that I'm afraid those roughnecks got a bit carried away tossing you about."

"I loved it." She sighed contentedly. "It was like flying."

"I know you did," he said tenderly, "That's why I didn't have the heart to step in and put an end to it. You were like a bit of thistledown whirling out of control on the dance floor tonight."

"I think I looked quite like one of your Texas cowgirls," Sheena said, looking down happily at her scarlet prairie skirt with its white cotton underskirt and matching off-the-shoulder blouse. Even her small cream leather boots looked quite satisfyingly western.

"Sorry, love, I can't agree. You look more like my wild gypsy lass than ever." His face abruptly lost its gentle, teasing expression. "I didn't see you indulging in any sotto voce machinations. I gather you're abandoning your plan to escape my evil clutches?"

"Of course not," she asserted sturdily, her brow wrinkling in a frown. "I have every intention of escaping. I just decided to do it tomorrow."

"I see. A very wise decision, my dear Scarlett. You just keep on thinking that way." He stopped in the middle of the dance floor. "Now, I think we'd better get you home while you're still floating on that pink cloud."

"All right," Sheena said agreeably. "But what about Nick?" Rand was propelling her steadily toward the door, and she looked over her shoulder trying to search out that raven head among the dancers.

"I told Nick that I'd take you home in the jeep and for him to catch a ride back to Crescent Creek with one of the men," Rand said. They passed outdoors into the surprisingly cool night.

"I like Nick," she confided, as she did a half step to keep up with him.

"All women like Nick." They reached the yellow jeep, and Rand swung her up into the passenger seat, then walked around the jeep and slipped lithely behind the wheel. "Now, hush up, and let me get you back to the Triple X before the euphoria turns into a very bad head."

She shot him an indignant glance and was about to make a cutting rejoiner when he took off with an explosive propulsion that almost rivaled O'Brien's.

She was smugly triumphant when they did reach the ranch, for she was still as marvelously uplifted as when they had left the dance. Couldn't the man tell the difference between being tipsy and sheer good spirits? If she was a trifle dizzy when he lifted her down from the jeep, she felt sure it was only the sudden cessation of motion after their wild, careening drive over the rough terrain.

Rand steadied her against his warm, hard body for a moment before he lifted her in his arms and carried her into the house.

"I can walk," she protested.

"I know," Rand said soothingly. "I just like to hold you. Okay?"

"Okay," Sheena said. Her head fell contentedly on his shoulder. It seemed a perfectly appropriate answer. She liked to hold him, too.

Sheena was vaguely conscious of being placed on the crisp eyelet coverlet of the double bed in the master bedroom. Then Rand's hands were busy loosening and removing her clothes. She heard him swear once as he pulled at one stubborn cream boot, but then it was free, and she was left in peace for a time.

It was uncomfortably cool on the cotton bedspread, she thought crossly, so she turned on her side and huddled in a ball. She felt her body being moved as the covers on which she was lying were drawn back. Then a warm, strong body that was already endearingly familiar was in bed with her, and Rand folded her securely in his arms, sharing his warmth. He pulled the covers over both of them, his lips pressing lazy kisses on her temple.

"Go to sleep, love," he whispered. "You've flown long and hard, it's time to return to the nest."

Sheena cuddled closer, her lips buried in the warm hollow of his throat. "Was I a lark tonight?" she asked drowsily, barely conscious of uttering the words.

Rand's arm tightened around her. "Oh, yes," he said with an odd huskiness in his voice. "God, yes. You were a magnificent lark, sweetheart."

"Good," she said contentedly, as she felt the warm throb of his pulse against her cheek lulling her into the comforting darkness of sleep.

The first movements were as gentle and soft as the fine Irish rain, and she sighed with contentment as she felt her thighs parted and Rand's magical hands caressing and toying with the very heart of her. He was infinitely slow and easy, not demanding anything of her but her submission. She was almost asleep again when she felt him enter her with painstaking carefulness, his warm hardness stretching and filling her with the urgency of his need.

She opened her eyes slowly and made a little sound that reflected both her surprise and contentment. Rand was bending over her, an expression of almost glazed intentness on his face. At her exclamation, he looked down at her with a smile that took her breath away with its loving tenderness.

"Shh," he crooned softly. "Just relax, love. I'll do it all." He lowered his lips to kiss her with fairylike lightness. "I didn't want to disturb you, but I found I couldn't go to sleep without returning to *my* nest." He made a movement with his hips that caused her to catch her breath and was more than self-explanatory.

Then with a delicacy that Rand had never before shown her in their wild, almost desperate lovemaking, he began to move. Each thrust was as easy and gentle as the first, and she gradually relaxed and obeyed his instructions and left it up to him. She was halfway between waking and sleep, and it was deliciously sensual to be moved and stroked and praised while Rand took his own pleasure with her body.

But suddenly it wasn't enough. Sheena began to move against him with a frantic urgency that caused him to clutch her to him in a wild flurry of passion that erupted into a feverish climax.

"Sweet lovely lark," he said afterward, as he tucked the sheet around her and settled her possessively in his embrace. He was stroking her satin back with a soothing gentleness, and she felt his lashes oddly wet against her cheek. "*My* lark."

She nodded drowsily and went peacefully back to sleep.

The noon sun was streaming through the frilly eyelet curtains when Sheena next opened her eyes. She was vaguely conscious of an uneasy sensation of loneliness, of something not as it should be. Then she realized that she was no longer wrapped in Rand's arms, which had held her so tightly through the night. She looked in sudden panic at the pillow next to hers, but only a slight indentation recalled his presence. She sat upright, then groaned aloud as she felt pains shooting through her head. Her hands went to her temples, and she rubbed them ruefully. So much for her confidence that she could hold her drinks, she thought wryly. What was that odd term Rand had used? Oh, yes, white lightning.

Her discomfort and sense of desertion were partially dispelled when she noticed the open bedroom door and heard the muffled sound of water running through the pipes. Rand must be in the shower, she realized, with a ridiculous sense of relief. She leaned back on the pillow and allowed herself to relax.

How foolish to fly into a panic just because Rand had not been there when she awoke, she thought. She had opened her eyes every day of her twenty-two years to a world with no Rand Challon. Yet it had taken only two days for her to realize how empty and meaningless her future would be without him beside her every morning.

Her gaze traveled lazily about the room, finding it just as pleasant as she had thought the previous afternoon. It was not nearly as luxurious as Rand's cabin in Canada, but it had a simple hominess that was enhanced by the polished oak floors and the slightly worn blue wing chair in the far corner of the room. The only furniture besides the double bed was the maple chest of drawers beside the door and a small matching bedside table.

It was as her eyes were glancing carelessly at the bedside table that her attention was caught by the glass of water with the white card with her name scrawled in bold black letters propped against it. Directly below it was a pretty white plastic compact with gold embossing on it, and she reached over and picked it up curiously. It must be a gift from Rand, but this cheap, trinket was not the type of present that Challon would choose, she thought in puzzlement.

It was only when she flipped open the lid that she understood. She stared blankly at the rows of tiny pink pills arranged in neat circles, and color swiftly flooded her face. She uttered a low, involuntary moan of distress. The shock was like a blow when she realized the cold, cynical message inherent in Rand's gift of the pills.

She shook her head dazedly as she swung her legs to the side of the bed and stood up. The pill. She had been so involved in the sheer sensual ecstasy of Rand's lovemaking that she had not given a thought to the possible ramifications. It seemed that Rand had not been similarly carried away, she thought numbly, and she hurriedly pulled on jeans and a white oxford cloth shirt. He had obviously wanted to protect himself from the possible results of their union.

She felt a chill of desolation sweep over her as she carelessly slipped on a pair of loafers and ran from the room and down the stairs without even taking a comb to her hair.

She ran down the porch steps and started walking blindly, her emotions in a confused turmoil. She didn't know herself why Rand's rejection of a possible child by her filled her with such pain. She knew their relationship might be an ephemeral one at best. She herself had told Rand that she would leave at the first opportunity. It was only reasonable that he would not want to take any chances that a pregnancy might result from a brief affair. Her mind could accept Challon's reasoning, but her emotions recoiled with an instinctive revulsion at the cool emotionlessness of Rand's action.

She walked for a long time, not even noticing the heat of the strong afternoon sun on her uncovered head or the distance that she'd wandered from the house. It was only when she happened on a small inviting pond surrounded by huge weeping willows that she realized how hot and tired she'd become. It was such a lovely, peaceful spot, she thought, as she sat down in the long grass bordering the bank. The water in the pond was deep green, and there were white water lilies floating on its dark surface like perfect jewels in a velvet display case. The weeping willows' profusion of lacy fronds trailed the ground and danced gracefully with every vagrant breeze.

She took a deep breath and closed her eyes, letting the warm sun bathe her in its soothing balm and relax the tension that was gripping her. She sat there for a long time, listening to the whoosh of the breeze through the willows and the soft, throaty sound of the birds. She deliberately blocked out the unhappy thoughts that were rioting through her mind and disturbing the serenity of the moment and strove to enjoy the beauty around her.

Presently, tempted by the hot sun and the solitude, she stripped off her clothes and entered the emerald water of the pond. The water was cold and silky against her hot flesh, and she remained there longer than she had intended. She swam lazily among the water-lily pads, then dreamily floated and watched the reflection of the willow fronds on the water.

When she reluctantly climbed back on the bank, the sun was a good deal lower in the sky. It took very little time for the sun to dry the excess moisture from her body, and then she leisurely donned her jeans and shirt. She stretched out on the bank to run her fingers through her wet, curly mop and allowed the sun to dry it quickly into a wild, glossy aureole about her head.

"Isn't that just like a woman. We're scouring the countryside for you, and you're out taking a sunbath."

Sheena sat up, startled. Nick O'Brien was sitting indolently on the back of a tall black stallion, perhaps ten yards away. One jean-clad leg was crossed casually over the pommel as he looked down at her, a grin on his face. He was wearing a bright blue shirt that deepened his aquamarine eyes to almost turquoise.

Sheena was abruptly conscious of her tousled hair and the revealing way her blouse was clinging to her still moist skin. "I'm not sunbathing," she protested. "I was just sitting here thinking."

He shook his head reprovingly, then took his leg from the pommel and slid from the saddle. "Meanwhile, Rand has been going crazy looking for you." He tossed the reins over the horse's head. "He was planning on calling out all the hands from Crescent Creek if we hadn't found you by sundown." He took a rifle from the holster on the saddle and fired three shots in rapid succession before replacing it in the holster.

"What was that all about?" Sheena asked, her dark eyes wide with surprise.

"Just a signal to let Rand know where we are." Nick strolled over to her and sat down beside her on the grass. He crossed his legs Indian fashion. "Now we wait. He should be here soon. He's searching the south quadrant."

"I'm sorry to have put you to this unnecessary trouble," Sheena said politely. "I was in no danger."

O'Brien gave her a long, skeptical look. "I think that we both know that Rand wasn't worried about any physical danger to you. He thought you had run away from him."

Sheena felt the swift color rise to her cheeks. "I guess that means that he told you about his little kidnapping scheme," she said, not looking at him. "I suppose you won't help me, either. I've never known anyone to have so many willing accomplices."

"That should tell you something about the man," he said quietly. "Is it likely that he could inspire such loyalty if he wasn't a damn decent human being?"

"Oh, I just don't know," Sheena said despairingly, running her hand through her hair. "I don't know what's right or wrong anymore, or who to trust."

"That's easy," O'Brien said, his gaze fixed gravely on her face. "Trust Rand, you'll never regret it."

"You're very loyal to him. Rand said you would be."

"We've been through a few tough spots together. When the chips are down, you get to know who your friends are." He plucked a long strand of grass and chewed it thoughtfully. "I guess Rand told you that I'm something of a freak," he said slowly. There was something lost and lonely in the depths of his eyes.

Sheena felt a surge of sympathy that was almost maternal. "He told me that you were something of a genius," she said gently.

His lips curved cynically. "One term is as good as another. I was having some pretty heavy adjustment problems when Rand appeared on the scene two years ago. He helped me get my head together, and I owe him a hell of a debt."

"I can see how you would feel that way," Sheena said quietly. "I believe in the payment of debts, too. That's one of the problems."

"So I understand," O'Brien said. "But if Rand has an objection, you can be damn sure it's a valid one. Like I said, trust him, Sheena."

"You're wasting your breath, Nick," Challon said harshly. "The lady prefers her comfortable little cocoon. She's not about to try thinking for herself."

O'Brien and Sheena both turned startled eyes to the grim figure on the chestnut mare. In beige suede pants and tan-and-cream-checked shirt, Rand looked a study in browns against the shiny coat of the horse. They had been so engrossed in their conversation, they had not been aware of Rand's approach.

Challon dismounted swiftly, flipped the reins over the horse's head, and strode toward them, bitterness and determination in every line of his powerful body. His lion eyes were flickering with anger as he looked down at them. Sheena instinctively made an involuntary movement of withdrawal, and Rand's lips tightened to a hard line as he noticed the gesture.

"You can go back to the ranch now, Nick," he said tersely. "I'll take over from here."

O'Brien stood up slowly, his eyes on Challon's stony face. "Simmer down, Rand," he said quietly. "She's all mixed up. She didn't mean to worry you."

"Didn't she?" Rand asked. "Then Sheena seems to have an amazing talent for putting me through hell. Stay out of it, Nick."

O'Brien shrugged. "Whatever you say. It's your affair." He sauntered over to the black stallion and mounted lithely.

"Exactly," Challon said grimly, glancing down at Sheena. "I'm glad you understand that."

"I'll be at Crescent Creek if you need me," Nick said, then wheeled the black. He looked over his shoulder, a glint of mischief shimmering in his eyes. "I believe I just may stick around for a while. Things are beginning to get interesting." Then with a mocking wave of his hand, he kicked the stallion into a gallop.

Eight

Challon turned immediately back to Sheena and looked down at her with profound displeasure. "I see that you've managed to catch Nick in the snare of those big black eyes," he snapped irritably. "I've never seen him so protective where a woman's concerned."

Sheena had been sitting back on her heels in a half kneeling position, but now she started to struggle to her feet. "He's a very good friend to you," she commented quietly. "And I have no need of his protection. I can take care of myself."

Rand pushed her back down in her former position. "Sit down," he ordered tersely. "I have a few words to say to you." The last words were ominously grim, as was the expression on his face. He dropped down on his knees facing her and took her shoulders in a grip of pure iron. "If you ever do this to me again, I won't be responsible for my actions," he said tightly. "I won't be put through this hell again. Do you understand me, Sheena?"

She nodded, her mouth pouting sulkily. "I'm sure you would enjoy punishing me very much," she said, her dark eyes flashing. "It's not my fault you chose to go tearing around the countryside looking for me. The hell was of your own making, Rand Challon."

"I'm well aware of that. I started constructing it some five years ago when I first saw you, Sheena, and I've accepted a certain amount of mental harassment as going with the territory. But I'll be damned if I'll let you do this to me. If you don't give me your promise not to try to run away again, I'll lock you up."

She tried futilely to shrug off his hold. "I wasn't trying to run away," she said defiantly. "i would have made a much better job of it if I had been. I'm not stupid, Rand."

"No, you're very bright," he agreed. "That doesn't preclude you being the most muddleheaded, the most stubborn, the most—"

"You don't have to go on," she interrupted furiously. "I think I understand what you think of me now. Well, you don't have to continue our association if I'm such a trial to you. You can always let me go."

He gave her an exasperated shake. "You know better than that. You belong to me," he said forcefully.

"I don't belong to anyone," she said, her voice rising with anger. "This isn't the Dark Ages, and I'm certainly not a humble serf awaiting your pleasure. You may have all the money in the world, but you can't buy me, Rand!"

"There are other ways of buying people than with money, Sheena," Challon retorted. "I've invested five years and considerable emotional wear and tear on you. When you can say the same, I'll grant that you own a considerable piece of me, too."

"You can feel quite safe in that offer," Sheena said bitterly. "You know as well as I that what we have is fleeting at best. You've made that quite clear."

Rand cursed under his breath. "That's the most idiotic thing you've ever said to me. You're the one who is afraid of committing yourself. I asked you to marry me, didn't I?"

"A temporary aberration, no doubt," she snapped. "A fitting conclusion to your little fantasy about me. However, if it comes down to brass tacks, you're very much the realist, aren't you, Rand?"

"I suppose you know what you're talking about, but I certainly don't. What more do you want from me, for God's sake!"

"I don't want anything from you!" Sheena cried, her dark eyes bright with rage and unhappiness. "Why don't you just go away and let me alone?"

"Because I'm not about to let you get away with this crazy nonsense you've been giving me. Not without getting to the bottom of it. Now will you tell me why you're so damn upset?"

Sheena's lips tightened stubbornly, her dark eyes mutinous.

Rand's eyes narrowed to catlike slits. "I suppose I'll have to work it out for myself," he said slowly. "But it's not going to make me any more pleased with you, Sheena. If you weren't running away from me, why did you take off like that?"

Sheena moistened her lips nervously. She would have rather faced Rand's anger than this formidable analytical ruthlessness. "I just wanted to get away and think for a little while," she said evasively. "How was I to know you'd go haring all over the Rio Grand valley looking for me?"

"You knew," he said slowly, searching her face keenly. "But I think you were too upset to care. Now I wonder what could have put you into such a tailspin?"

Sheena could almost hear the wheels go around behind the intentness of Rand's expression, and she looked away suddenly, color flooding her cheeks. It was too much to expect that Rand would not note and correlate that revealing surge of color.

"Well, I'll be damned," Rand said blankly. "It was the pills."

Sheena stubbornly refused to answer, her gaze fastened on the top button of his shirt.

"I could murder you," he grated, his hands tightening on her shoulders. "Do you mean that I've wasted an entire afternoon searching to hell and gone because of those damn pills? Did it ever occur to you to discuss the issue with me instead of running off like a confused child?"

"There wasn't anything to discuss," she said tartly. "Your actions were fairly self-explanatory. Was that why Dr. Knowleton was so thorough in his examination?"

Challon shook his head. "He thought you were already pregnant. When you were ill yesterday, he thought quite probably that it was morning sickness. He knew how wild I was about you. He was practically flabbergasted when he discovered you weren't my mistress already."

"So he gave you the pills," Sheena said acidly. "You're surrounded by such considerate friends, Rand. They're all trying to protect you from the penalties of your folly."

"I asked him for the pills, damn it!" he said harshly. "I had the idiotic idea that you were the one who needed the protection. It's your body that will bear our child, Sheena. I have no right to take that freedom of choice from you." His lips curved cynically. "Hell, it may be too late already, but I thought I'd be noble and give you the means to protect yourself if you chose to accept it." A frown darkened his face, and his eyes turned flinty. "You little fool, don't you realize how tempting it would be for me to just let nature take its course? You'd find it pretty well impossible to leave me if you were pregnant. It would simplify the entire situation. But I didn't want you that way, damn it. I wanted you to come to me freely without that particular type of physical blackmail."

"I'm sorry, I didn't understand," Sheena said huskily, her dark eyes wide and stricken. "I just thought you didn't want the responsibility."

Challon's expression lost none of its hardness. "You never do understand, and you never give me the benefit of a doubt." He grinned mirthlessly. "Good Lord, I even thought you'd be grateful to me! How stupid can I get?"

Sheena felt the tears brim helplessly as she gazed at the bitterness that was carved into Challon's expression. For a moment, there was a flicker in the depths of Rand's golden eyes that reflected an odd hurt. Then there was nothing but a hard ruthlessness.

He released her abruptly and swiftly rose to his feet. "Well, it seems that I was wrong," he said harshly. "If you think I'm afraid to make that particular commitment, there's only one way to prove you wrong." Rapidly he began unbuttoning his shirt. He stripped it off and threw it carelessly to the ground, his bronze, muscular shoulders shimmering like copper in the late afternoon sunlight. "And I'm fully prepared to start right now!"

"What are you going to do?" Sheena cried, startled, as he swooped down and scooped her up in his arms. Her heart was beating rapidly with fear and a strange excitement as she clung to Rand's naked shoulders. He strode rapidly toward the pond. "Rand! Let me down!"

"Not before I've demonstrated my willingness to meet the test," he said mockingly. "I wouldn't think of disappointing you."

"I said I was sorry," Sheena protested frantically. Rand was striding directly toward the pond, and she had a ghastly feeling that he was going to toss her in.

"I'm not. I intend to enjoy every minute of it."

They were both suddenly enveloped in a cloud of lacy fronds as Rand ducked beneath the branches of a huge weeping willow tree clinging to the bank of the pond. Then they were clear of the clinging leaves and surrounded with an almost twilight dimness. Rand put her down on a cushioned softness, which she vaguely identified as a bed of moss, and knelt beside her, his hands at the buttons of her blouse.

Sheena looked around her in incredulous bewilderment. The trailing fronds of the weeping willows formed a delicate, lacy curtain all around them, sealing them away from the world as completely as the closing of a bedroom door. The sun filtered through the branches intermittently, lighting the verdant dimness and painting dancing, shadowy patterns on the ground.

"It's like a world all its own," she said wonderingly. "I never dreamed this was here."

"When I was a kid, I used to run over to Green Willow Pond every chance I got. Laura never could see the attraction when Crescent Creek had so much property for me to roam. I never told her it was like having my own private sanctuary beneath every willow surrounding the pond. It was every kid's dream."

"So when you grew up, you bought the property," Sheena said softly, her eyes on his lean, hard face as she tried to imagine the wild, mischievous boy who had come here so many years before.

"I bought the property because it was a good investment," he said, looking up to meet her eyes. "Sentiment didn't enter into the picture."

"Didn't it?" Sheena asked gently, her dark eyes tender. "I think perhaps it did."

Challon shrugged. "Think what you like. You'll find I'm not known for being a romantic. I leave that to fey little Irish folksingers."

Sheena smothered a smile. What could be more impossibly romantic than his half a decade obsession with the mystique of one Sheena Reardon?

Challon had undone the last button of her shirt and was about to push the material from her shoulders when she put a hand on his hands to stop him. "Why are you doing this, Rand?" she asked quietly.

His lips twisted mockingly as he met her eyes. "We're going to make a baby, Sheena," he said coolly. "Or at least we're going to give it a damn good try. Will that satisfy your suspicions of me?"

"I never said that I wanted to get pregnant," Sheena said softly. "I know that I hurt you with my distrust of you, but this isn't the way to punish me, Rand. You'll only regret it later."

"Probably," he admitted, brushing her hands aside and slipping the shirt from her shoulders. "But it's too late to think about that. I couldn't stop now if I tried."

For the first time Sheena noticed the slight tremble of Challon's hands, and the trip-hammer pulse in his temple that belied the coolness of his manner. His eyes became warmly intent as they moved from her face to the full curve of her naked breasts. He drew a deep, unsteady breath as his hands reached out to gently cup her warm softness.

"Maybe I was just looking for an excuse," he said hoarsely, leaning forward so that his lips were only a breath away. Each soft word resulted in a tiny kiss as he continued. "I've been wanting you so much all day, it's like being in a fever. Perhaps I'm the one who's the addict."

Sheena was trembling so much that she could barely hide the effect of his nearness, and her voice was choked and breathless. "You're not angry anymore?"

Rand shook his head, each motion a brushing caress on her lips. "It would take a stronger man than I am to remain angry at a moment like this, dove. All I can think of is seeing you lying naked before me on this bed of moss. God, I want that!" His thumbs were gently stroking her nipples, and Sheena could feel her body responding, as much from the evocative effect of his words as his gentle manipulations.

She looked up at him, her eyes oddly grave. "I think I want that, too," she said huskily. She swayed closer to his virile strength as if he were a magnet that controlled her very being. Perhaps he was, she thought dazedly, as she slid her arms around his waist and pressed her naked breasts to his hard, corded chest. He had only to touch her to start this throbbing ache in her loins.

A violent shudder shook him as he felt her nipples harden with eagerness as they brushed against his tawny, hair-roughened chest. "You're sure?" he asked raggedly, pulling her closer to him. "I'll try to protect you, but I can't guarantee anything. I go crazy when I'm loving you."

She nestled closer, pressing little kisses on the smooth, warm flesh of his shoulder. "I'm sure," she said breathlessly, as his hands began tracing sensual patterns at the base of her spine. "You don't have to protect me. I don't care."

"God, little dove, neither do I!" Rand covered her lips with a frantic hunger that she met with equal passion. His tongue invaded her with hot urgency, exploring and playing with her own until they were both shaking and breathless with need. His hands were working with odd clumsiness at the front fastening of her jeans, and she found that she was not much better as she unfastened his belt.

"I'll do it, love," he said taking her hands away from his waist. "I want this to last a long time, and your hands on me make me wild." He quickly stripped her of her jeans and pushed her back on the bed of moss so that she was lying full length before him, her long gypsy curls framing her face and her tiny silken body arching with ardent eagerness, pleading for his caresses.

"Hell, just looking at you makes me wild." He placed a trembling hand on her soft belly and began a gentle, massaging motion that caused her to arch helplessly against the electric touch. "You're so small," he said wonderingly. "How is it that you can hold me?"

He lowered his head to brush his lips where his hand had been caressing. "You're all softness and warmth and sweet-smelling woman." His tongue darted out to stroke her sensitive flesh, and she inhaled sharply as her body quivered with response. "I love everything about you, do you know that? Even the taste of you turns me on." His lips traveled up to the peaks of her waiting breasts and nibbled at the engorged nipples lazily.

Sheena was not feeling a similar leisureliness. Every

touch of his hands was like a galvanic shock; each teasing bite at her sensitive nipples was causing a fever that generated a molten ache in every limb. She began to pant and make little moaning sounds deep in her throat, and he raised his head and smiled at her with almost savage pleasure before resuming his tormenting loveplay.

She felt as if she were about to go up in flames, and she bit her lower lip in frustration at the maddening slowness of his teasing arousal. Rand might have the experience and control to indulge in this type of sensual game, but she did not. Her hands clutched at his wide, muscular shoulders feverishly, and her nails unconsciously scored him with the urgency of her need.

He laughed deep in his throat and sat back on his heels, his golden eyes dancing with exultant amusement. "That's right. Put your marks on me, little kitten. I want to look at them later and remember how you looked at this moment." He leisurely parted her thighs so that she was open and vulnerable to his every whim, and he looked down at her, his eyes glazed to a dark amber. "You look like a sacrifice to an ancient pagan god," he said thickly, his fingers stroking her inner thigh.

But Sheena couldn't bear any more. Rand was evidently going to continue playing with her until she was out of her mind with hunger. That is, if she didn't do something to rock his control, she thought mischievously.

With one swift movement, she closed her thighs on his hand, capturing him in her soft warmth. At the same time, she gracefully sat up and smiled at him alluringly. "But I have no desire to be a sacrifice," she said throatily, then slowly got to her knees. "The role is much too submissive, I'd rather be the high priestess."

She moved closer to him and rubbed her breasts against his chest like a sensuous cat, then lowered her lips to nibble delicately at his shoulder. "I'll be very careful not to use my hands on you," she said demurely. "I wouldn't want to drive you wild, would I?"

She then proceeded to do just that. Her teeth and tongue moved to his hard male nipples and gave them the same teasing attention that he'd accorded her. He obviously found it just as arousing as she had, for she could feel his heartbeat accelerate. Her head moved down to his hard stomach, and she felt his muscles knot with tension as her lips brushed against him. When her warm tongue darted out teasingly to stroke his navel, he decided he had reached the limit of his patience.

With a groan that was like the growl of a wild animal, he pushed her away from him onto her back. He tore at his clothes frantically until he was as naked and vulnerable as she was, then came into her with the passion of a hunger suppressed too long.

For an instant Sheena felt a quiver of fear at the almost painful thrust of his arousal, but then she was lost in a rhythm so fiery that she knew only its exultant throb. She could see Rand's face, stark and primitive with desire, above her. He was all golden power and beautiful naked aggression in the shadowy canopy of their leafy bower. She wondered dazedly if Adam had looked like this when he'd shown Eve a paradise more beautiful than Eden.

Then she couldn't think at all as the fantastic tension mounted until it was a shimmering silver cord binding them together in the most joyously primitive captivity known to man. Then the cord broke, shredding into ribbons of sensation that was as dazzling as the glittering cord itself.

They didn't leave the magical environs of the willow tree until the setting sun was a fiery ball in the west. Sheena couldn't remember any of the words that were spoken in those hours. She was vaguely aware of broken murmurs of need and assuagement as they flowed together innumerable times in an almost dreamlike pattern of molten desire. No words were necessary in that curiously timeless period where there was only the language of smooth, yearning flesh and warm, inviting glances.

It was only when Challon noticed Sheena give an involuntary shiver that shook her body even in the warm shelter of his arms, that he reluctantly put an end to their idyll. He pulled on his clothes slowly, his eyes fixed compulsively on her pale, languid body, which was now bathed eerily in the soft green glow evoked by the setting sun on the thick green foliage. "You look like a lovely alien from outer space," he said, watching her sit up lazily and begin to arrange her tousled hair into some sort of order.

"I feel like one, too," Sheena said dreamily, as she looked vaguely around for her clothes. She felt almost too deliciously weary to move, and she gave up looking for her clothes to gaze with frank enjoyment at Rand's swift, graceful movements as he donned his own garments. Watching the rippling muscles in his brawny shoulders as he pulled on his shirt, she felt a surge of familiar heat.

"Oh, no, you don't, love," Rand said, noting and comprehending the growing languor in her dark eyes. "No more until I get you home. I'm not having you develop a chill while I sate myself on that gorgeous body." He finished buttoning his shirt and then briskly hurried about collecting her discarded clothing, which he handed to her.

He bent down and gave her a swift, hard kiss. "I'm tempted to stay and watch you dress, but I don't trust my willpower. I'll water the mare while you remove temptation from my path." With another quick kiss, he parted the long, lacy fronds and strode out of the haven beneath the willows.

Sheena sat still for a brief moment and then started hurriedly to dress. She shivered, suddenly conscious of how cool it had become. For some reason when Rand had left, he had seemed to take all the vibrant warmth with him. The dark shadows and strange, eerie glow no longer appeared beautiful but silently menacing.

Sheena pulled on her jeans and white shirt, her hands moving swiftly on the zipper and buttons, and then looked around her for the brown loafers.

She spotted them by the root of the tree. Sinking back down on the ground, she slipped on the shoes. Then she rose to her knees and tucked her white blouse into her jeans. A sudden breeze disturbed the willow fronds, and she sat back on her heels, her gaze fixed on Rand's powerful silhouette at the bank of the pond some ten feet away. Standing by the chestnut's head, he looked like a painting of one of the colorful cowboy figures by Remington, she thought dreamily.

She rose to her knees again as she prepared to stand up. There was a sudden peculiar sound like the rattle of dry peas in a metal cup, and she froze in position, more in surprise than fear. She casually looked toward the direction from which the sound had come. Her body turned to a rigid block of ice as she faced the flat, triangular head and the evil, glowing eyes of a rattle-snake!

The snake was only a scant three feet away and almost on a level with her kneeling form; it was coiled to strike. The ominous rattle sounded again, and she gave a low moan of pure terror. Such a short time ago she had compared this spot to Eden, she remembered with panicky horror. How ironic that it was another serpent that was destroying their magic garden as well.

"Sheena!"

It was Rand's voice, but he was outside the leafy enclosure and seemed a million miles away. Only she and the swaying white and tan monster existed in this world. The rattle sounded again, and Sheena sobbed uncontrollably.

"Sheena, how far away is the snake?" Rand's voice was as commanding as a whiplash. How far away? He was practically in her arms. She had an instant of wondering how Rand had known about her predica-ment before she realized that he must have heard the telltale rattle and her own terrified cry.

"Sheena, damn it, speak to me! I can't see through these branches, and I can't charge blindly in there if it's close enough to strike. How far from you is it?"

"Three feet," she gasped, watching the flat head sway back and forth. No wonder the devil was personified as a snake. There was something so malevolent in its eyes.

She heard Rand swear, and then once again his voice roared. "I need to know the exact location. Do you hear me, Sheena? Tell me precisely where it is."

Her throat felt dry as cotton as she tried to force the words from her throat. "It's facing me, about three feet away. It's about six feet from the bank near the trunk of the tree."

"Good girl! Now don't move a muscle, do you hear?"

No danger of that, she thought almost hysterically. She was too terrified to breathe, much less move. The horror was magnified by the almost unbearable tension of wondering when the serpent would strike. For a crazy moment, she had an urge to make a motion that would precipitate the strike just to end the nightmare once and for all.

What happened next was infinitely worse than the terror that had gone before. With speed too blinding to follow, Rand suddenly appeared through the fronds behind the snake and grabbed it by the rattles and slung it forcefully against the willow tree! Sheena heard a sickening crack as the snake hit the tree, then with an equally forceful backward motion, Rand sent the body of the snake flying into the pond.

Sheena stared at him dazedly as he calmly wiped his hands on his tan suede pants, then turned around to face her. Her eyes were fixed on him with the same horror they had held when she was mesmerized by that ancient symbol of evil. Rand's expression darkened with concern as he saw her expression, and he took a swift step toward her.

"No!" The cry was almost a moan as Sheena leaped to

her feet and tore through the delicate foliage into the sunset brilliance of the outside world.

"Sheena!" Rand's voice thundered after her. She didn't stop until she reached the bank of the pond. She bent over, holding her stomach with both arms while she fought the nausea that was threatening to overcome her. She took several deep, steadying breaths, and the sickness gradually faded.

"Easy, little dove," Rand said gently, his hands closing on her tension-racked shoulders.

Sheena gave an outraged cry, like the sound of a spitting tiger, and whirled to face him. Her hand swung back, and she struck his cheek with all her might. "Damn you!" she shouted, her eyes dark with rage. "Damn you, Rand Challon! I could murder you!"

Her hands were beating at his chest with all her strength while Rand looked down at her with a dumbfounded expression on his face. "What the hell is wrong with you?" he roared, trying to ward off her blows without hurting her.

"What's wrong with me?" she cried, as she knotted one small fist and punched him fiercely in the stomach. "It's what's wrong with you! You're the stupidest, the cruelest, the most asinine man on the face of the earth. I hate everything about you! You're a terrible, terrible man!" She ended the diatribe with a swift, hard kick to his kneecap that caused him to utter a surprised yelp.

"You ought to be locked away with the other loonies so that you can't hurt yourself," she told him, unaware of the tears running down her cheeks. "What kind of daft chance was that for any man to take? You picked that snake up with your bare hands. What if he had bitten you? What if he had killed you, damn it?" She kicked him in the other kneecap. "It would have served you right for being such an idiot. I wish that it *had* killed you!"

He grabbed her firmly by the shoulders, trying to avoid her lethally accurate feet. "Listen to me, Sheena," he said earnestly. "It wasn't as dangerous as it looked.

The snake was probably sluggish from the evening coolness." He gave her a little shake. "I know about snakes, for God's sake. When I was a kid, we went on rattlesnake roundups in the hills every year."

"Not dangerous!" she raged, struggling to escape that steely grip. "I was there, remember? There was nothing sluggish about that rattlesnake! The only thing that was sluggish about the entire situation was that tiny little brain of yours." Noting how successfully he was evading her kicks, she lifted her knee, aiming at an extremely sensitive portion of his anatomy. It was a glancing blow but enough to cause him to utter a pained bellow and loosen his hold on her arms.

She broke away from him and was a full twenty yards away before he had recovered enough to pursue her. But then his pursuit was swift and ruthlessly efficient. She found herself neatly tackled and falling to the ground. The earth was jarringly hard despite its covering of long grass, and for an instant the fall shocked her into immobility. Rand took advantage of her weakness to pin her on her back with her arms above her head. He quickly mounted her supine body and shook the sun-bleached hair out of his eyes to look down at her.

"Let me go!" Sheena demanded, trying to wriggle away from him. She had recovered quickly once the first surprise was over, and her fury was only aggravated by the frustrating feeling of helplessness she was experiencing under Rand's weight. "You're not only an insane egomaniac, you're an abuser of helpless women!"

"Helpless! You damn near emasculated me. I'm not about to let you up until I find out what the hell is at the bottom of this." His golden eyes narrowed as he looked down into her distraught face and snapping black eyes. "Why are you so upset? I can understand that an experience like that would shake you up a bit, but this is out of all proportion."

She was stubbornly silent. Her only answer was the

redoubling of her efforts to escape from him. Let the idiot work it out for himself, she thought defiantly.

It seemed that he had, for a jubilant glint appeared in Rand's eyes, and his face lit up with the brilliance of his flashing smile. "You were worried about me," he said wonderingly. "You were scared to death that the rattlesnake would get me."

"Why should I be worried about a senseless, insensitive—"

"Why, indeed?" Rand mused. "Why would you be so upset that you nearly went crazy when you thought I was in danger? Why were you more afraid for me than you were for yourself?"

"I wasn't afraid for you! Why should I be afraid for anyone so completely witless as to pick up a striking rattlesnake with his bare hands?" Despite her anger, a convulsive shudder shook her at the memory.

"I think we both know the answer to that, don't we, dove?" he asked softly. His gaze was fastened searchingly on her face. "But that's not enough for me. I want the words."

Her lips tightened obstinately as she glared up at him.

"I guess I'll have to do it the hard way." He sighed regretfully, then his expression hardened. "I lied to you, you know. I knew damn well that snake was capable of striking. I wasn't really worried about him getting my hand, but there was a possibility that he might strike at my throat as I swung him around. Snakebites that close to the heart are almost always fatal."

"Shut up!" The picture that his words evoked was terrifyingly vivid.

"Of course, it's not a hundred percent fatal if treated immediately," he went on. "But we're pretty well isolated here."

"You're a sadistic monster," she hissed. She had stopped struggling, but her eyes were blazing ebony fire into his face.

"I want the words," he said with steely determination.

"Would you like me to go into the symptoms of snake-bite?"

"No!" she cried hoarsely, her eyes tortured in her pale face. "Why are you doing this to me?"

"I want the words, Sheena," he said relentlessly. "Give me the words."

"Damn it, I love you!" she shouted. "Now will you please shut up?"

Rand chuckled exultantly. "I'd be delighted, sweetheart," he said joyously, and his lips covered hers in a kiss of honeyed sweetness.

His lips were so warm, so alive, and his arms slipping around her were all vibrant strength. Without conscious thought, her arms slid over his shoulders to the curly hair at the nape of his neck. Everything about him was so wonderfully, vividly alive, and he had risked that life with such careless disregard that she wanted to kill him.

"You're so damn stupid," she said huskily, when he lifted his lips from hers. "You had no right to take such a chance." How could she tell him how she felt when she had seen him handle that deadly reptile? It was as if her world had been ripped from its axis and sent spinning into outer space. All the old values and loyalties had burned into oblivion at the realization that Rand could be taken from her just as Rory had. She had known with a primitive, blinding certainty that Rand Challon was the mainspring of her existence, and if he had died, there would be nothing left.

"Yes, I know, love," he said soothingly, his hand smoothing her tousled curls back from her face. "I'm stupid and cruel and everything you say. Now will you stop crying?"

Her body was shaking with sobs, and her cheeks were wet with tears. "You had no right," she repeated brokenly. "No right at all."

He rolled over, taking her with him so that they lay side by side in the grass. He cuddled her gently, his hands stroking the curve of her back soothingly. "God,

I'm sorry, dove," he whispered huskily. "I was a bastard to put you through that, but I have my insecurities, too. I needed you to tell me that you loved me."

"Well, I hope you're satisfied." Sheena sniffed indignantly, rubbing her wet cheeks on his crisp cotton shirt. "You got your own way and nearly gave me a nervous breakdown. I wouldn't have put it past you to have arranged this whole thing."

"I hate to disappoint you, but that would have been beyond even my capabilities." Rand chuckled. "And I assure you, I wouldn't want you to go through that again even to gain me an advantage. I nearly had a heart attack when I saw you waltzing eye to eye with that rattler."

She shivered and nestled closer to him. "At least I didn't play crack the whip with it," she said tartly. She closed her eyes in rejection of that ghastly memory. "I don't want to think about it anymore."

"Right. I'd rather move on to more important matters anyway. When are you going to marry me?"

He was the most impossibly ruthless man she had ever run across, Sheena thought crossly. He was following up on her admission with his usual blunt determination, hoping to conquer all resistance in her present weakened state. Well, he had already gained all the victory he was going to that day. There was no way she was going to tell him that he had won hands down and that she would follow him barefoot around the world if he asked her to. She would save that for a time when he was not quite so satisfied with himself.

Sheena pushed him away and sat up. She carefully dusted herself off before answering him. "I don't recall that the situation has changed. Why should I suddenly decide to marry you just because I've discovered what a reckless idiot you can be? I should think that would be an exceptionally weighty argument against it."

He sat up, also brushing the dust from his clothes. He appeared not at all upset by her refusal as he stood up and pulled her to her feet. His expression was eminently satisfied, and his golden eyes held only a tender amusement as he took her hand in his and led her toward the chestnut mare at the bank. "You're a stubborn antagonist, Sheena Reardon," he said softly, his voice like warm velvet. "I won't push you any more today, love. I've gained enough ground to more than satisfy me."

He mounted the chestnut swiftly and then reached down to swing her up in front of him. He gave her a lingering kiss on the nape of her neck that caused her heart to start thumping like a tom-tom. "But we both know that I'm winning, don't we, love?" he whispered hoarsely. "The battle's almost over."

Sheena turned to look at him over her shoulder. There was no triumph in his face at that moment, and she felt her throat tighten with tears at what she did see there. There was loving tenderness and joy and the glowing eagerness of a little boy who was about to receive the blue ribbon for a race well run. God, he was so dear! She heard Rand's low chuckle beneath her ear as his arms tightened about her and he kicked the chestnut mare into a canter.

Nine

"You know, of course, that your shameless seduction of my person is not going to exempt you from a thorough tongue-lashing for running off," Rand pronounced, his darting tongue teasing her ear and belying the sternness of his tone. "Besides the fact that you turned me into a raving maniac, you might consider what might have resulted if you'd had to dispose of our rattler friend on your own."

Sheena settled herself more securely on the chestnut mare, trying to ignore the teasing provocation of Rand's exploring hands. He had displayed the exuberance of a naughty boy on the ride home to the ranch, and she hadn't had the heart to quench his bounding good spirits. "Actually, I might have done quite well on my own," she said loftily. "If you hadn't come in just at that moment, I was planning on singing to it."

"Singing!"

"Why not? If Indian cobras respond to music, why not American rattlesnakes?"

"Sheena, my love, I find your throaty little voice utterly enchanting," Rand said dryly. "But somehow I doubt that the rattlesnake would have been equally appreciative. I would suggest that next time you decide to go on a nature trek that you take a gun."

Sheena glanced down at the rifle lodged in the holster on the saddle. "Why didn't you use *your* gun instead of taking such a terrible chance?" she asked.

"I couldn't risk the bullet passing through the snake and hitting you." His hand had unbuttoned the middle two buttons of her shirt, and as he spoke one hand slipped inside to cup her bare breast in his hard palm.

"Rand!" she protested, inhaling deeply. The sudden caress sent a flood of heat surging through her. "Will you stop that?"

"Nope," he murmured, biting at her earlobe teasingly. "I never realized that riding a horse could be such an erotic experience. I had my eye on a little Arabian mare to buy for you, but I think we may ride tandem all the time." His thumb and forefinger were lazily kneading her nipple. "Did I tell you that I love the way your breasts just fit into my hands?"

"No." Sheena almost choked as she felt the familiar languid ache begin in her loins. "I don't believe you did." Then taking a deep breath, "Rand, I told you to stop that!"

"Why?" he asked innocently. "It's very obvious that you like it." His thumb flicked at the button-hard nipple teasingly, and Sheena felt a shudder of desire run through her.

"Rand, if you don't stop that, I'll get off and walk," Sheena said with a firmness born of desperation. She could see right now that Rand's penchant for casual fondling was going to pose myriad problems in their relationship. One of which being that she liked it far too much.

"Oh, very well." Rand sighed resignedly as he reluctantly removed his hand and buttoned her shirt. "It might be worth it at that to call your bluff," he said wistfully. "The house is just over the rise, and you wouldn't have very far to walk. It's not even dark yet."

"How very gallant." Sheena snorted indignantly. "It's not difficult to see where your priorities lie, Rand Challon."

"I did warn you about my insatiable lust," Rand murmured, as he massaged her jean-covered abdomen.

It was a comparatively safe form of petting, and Sheena found it very soothing. She leaned back against Rand's hard body and relaxed. "I've noticed that you do have tendencies in that direction. However, I think I've demonstrated that I can more than handle any demands you might make."

"Really?" Rand asked. "You think your recently acquired expertise qualifies you to that extent?"

"Why not?" Sheena asked airily. "I haven't observed any—Rand!"

Rand's hand had dipped suddenly beneath the waistband of her jeans and was resting on her soft bare belly, his thumb plunging erotically into her navel.

Challon burst into whoops of laughter, rocking back and forth on the chestnut mare until she thought they would both fall off. When he had finally controlled his amusement to a degree, he removed his hand and gave her an affectionate hug.

"Sorry, love," he said, his voice still threaded with laughter. "I couldn't resist it. I'll be good."

Now he'd be good! It was a fairly safe promise, she thought, since they had topped the rise and the house was only a few minutes away.

Abruptly she felt Rand's body stiffening against her like a lion scenting danger, and she looked around at him curiously. In the violet twilight dimness, all the amusement had been wiped from his face, and his features had taken on a wary hardness.

"What is it?" she asked, startled.

"It seems we have visitors."

Sheena followed his narrowed gaze to the small dark

green Datsun parked before the front porch of the house.

"You're not expecting anyone?" Sheena asked uneasily.

Rand shook his head. "I left orders that we *weren't* to be disturbed by anyone from Crescent Creek," he said, kicking the chestnut into a canter.

They reined up by the hitching rail in front of the house. Both the driver and the passenger doors of the green Datsun suddenly opened, and Sheena gasped, feeling almost dizzy with shock. There was no mistaking the square, powerful figure of Donal O'Shea and the lithe grace of Sean Reilly.

"Uncle Donal!" she exclaimed, as the two men slammed the car doors and strode purposefully toward them.

"Hello, Sheena, darlin'," O'Shea greeted her with the same casual warmth as if he'd seen her just the day before. "We've been waiting for you."

Challon's arms tightened around her involuntarily before he gained control of his reflexes. Then with utmost deliberation, he released her, dismounted swiftly, and lifted her from the horse to the ground.

"I wasn't expecting you so soon, O'Shea," he said, tying the reins to the hitching rail. "You moved faster than I thought you would. I thought you might spend a bit of time exploring the Canadian possibility before you came here."

O'Shea shook his head, a gentle smile on his face. "I wouldn't underestimate you to that extent, Mr. Challon," he said softly. "You're a clever man. You wouldn't risk the lovely Miss Scott ruining your plans without moving at once to rectify the problem. I've had a man at Crescent Creek for the past two weeks. When you transferred all the personnel here to the main headquarters, it was a fairly simple assumption that you'd be bringing Sheena here."

"Uncle Donal, what are you doing here?" Sheena asked dazedly. The two Irishmen in their dark tweed business suits looked definitely out of place in the bucolic surroundings, she noticed absently, as they came to a halt a few yards from them.

O'Shea shot her a surprised glance as if he'd forgotten she was there. "Why I've come to take you home, Sheena," he said genially. "I understand that you've been ill, but you're looking rosy as a child now. There's no reason at all for you not to resume your engagements. You'll be glad to know that the benefit concert is a complete sell-out."

"You didn't cancel it?" Sheena asked, her eyes widening incredulously. She had completely forgotten about the benefit in the weeks following her abduction. Now she recalled that the New York benefit was scheduled in only three days time.

O'Shea shook his head. "Of course not," he said briskly. "I know you better than that, Sheena. I knew that if it was at all possible, you'd wish to honor your obligations." He smiled. "You've never disappointed me before, love. Why should I mistrust you now?"

"She's not going back with you, O'Shea," Rand's steely voice cut through the air like a surgeon's scalpel. "Not now, not ever."

"But of course she is," O'Shea asserted. "You're reputed to be a very persuasive man where women are concerned, Challon, but Sheena knows where her duty lies. She may have been easy for you to lure away from her responsibilities when she was tired and ill, but you'll not find her so obliging now that Sean and I are here to support her."

"Support?" Rand asked. "That's an odd term to use for the type of subtle coercion you've used on Sheena all these years. It amazes me that she's never recognized your 'support' for what it is."

"My niece won't be influenced by your slander, Challon," O'Shea said gruffly. "She knows that I've always taken the greatest care of her. You've obviously mistaken her sweet, gentle nature for gullibility."

A smile of grim amusement curved Challon's lips. "I'm afraid I can't agree with your description of Sheena's meek, gentle personality," he said dryly. "Remind me to show you my bruises sometime. You know your niece even less than I thought."

"Stop it!" Sheena cried hoarsely, biting her lower lip in distress. "I won't have the two of you arguing and waltzing verbally about me as if I weren't even here. You're both treating me as if I were some sort of mindless doll!"

"Sorry, dove," Rand drawled. "I'm afraid this isn't the situation to exercise your newborn independence. Let me handle it."

There was a new element of wariness in O'Shea's expression as he said smoothly, "I didn't mean to upset you, darlin'. You know that I only want what's best for you."

Reilly spoke for the first time, a gentle smile on his handsome face. "Donal has always had your interests at heart, Sheena. You know that."

"Yes, I know that," Sheena said wearily. "I'm sorry I spoke rudely, Uncle Donal. It's just that your arrival was such a surprise that I'm a bit upset."

"It's perfectly understandable, love," O'Shea said soothingly. "I should have realized that you were still under a strain. Naturally I would have included you in the conversation if I'd known that you wished it." He grinned with appealing wryness and made a face. "I guess I've grown accustomed to trying to shelter you over the years."

Rand gave a snort of derision, and Sheena gave him a glance of extreme displeasure. His aggressive attitude wasn't helping the situation. She was already so confused and upset by the subtle pressure that her uncle was exerting that she was almost in tears. He had been her whole family for too long to just repudiate outright as Rand wanted her to do. Couldn't he understand how she was being torn between them?

"I do understand, Uncle Donal," she said. "It's just that there's been a change in the situation. We need to have a long discussion."

"To hell with discussions!" Rand said. "You're not going with him."

Sheena's lips thinned. "That's up to me, Rand. I'd appreciate it if you'd let me handle my own affairs as I see fit."

"You know that I'm always willing to listen, Sheena," O'Shea said earnestly. "Suppose you drive with us to Houston, and we'll talk on the way."

Rand muttered an impatient curse. "No way. I'm not trusting you out of my sight, Sheena. For God's sake, can't you see that he's manipulating you just as he's always done!"

"No, I can't see that!" Sheena cried, her dark eyes brimming with tears. "You've never understood that Uncle Donal isn't the villain that you think him. He's my family, and I care very much for him. He deserves better than the way you're treating him, damn it!"

O'Shea stepped quickly forward and took her in his arms, patting her shoulder comfortingly. "Easy, lass, don't get yourself all upset," he crooned soothingly. "He doesn't understand about us and what we've got to do. He wasn't there when Rory died." His large hand cupped her chin tenderly. "Remember how Rory held your hand until the very end, Sheena?"

Sheena felt a tearing pain shoot through her, and the tears were now running freely down her face. "No, he wasn't there," she said brokenly, her eyes dazed. "Rand wasn't there."

"You bastard!" Rand's voice was filled with such menace that it pierced even Sheena's misery. "My God, how the hell do you have the nerve to use her brother's death to whip her into line? Doesn't it even give you a twinge of guilt to use that particular weapon?"

"I don't know what you're talking about," O'Shea said coldly. "I don't believe you do either, Mr. Challon."

Challon's golden eyes narrowed dangerously. "But I do know, O'Shea," he said, his voice like molten steel. "I hoped I could spare Sheena the knowledge of what you are. She's had enough pain in her life without that cross to bear." He shook his tawny head in disbelief. "But you won't let her alone, will you? Rory's death wasn't enough. You want another sacrificial lamb to burn on the altar of your damn cause!"

"Rand!" Sheena's voice was a shocked gasp. "What are you saying?"

"I'm sorry, dove," he said quietly. "But it's got to end. I can't let him do this to you."

"You're a madman," O'Shea accused hoarsely, his square, powerful body oddly rigid. "Do you know what you're implying?"

"I'm not implying anything. I'm accusing you, O'Shea. You're as guilty of Rory Reardon's death as if you'd put a pistol to his head and pressed the trigger."

"Please, Rand, don't go on with this. You don't know what you're talking about," Sheena said huskily. "Uncle Donal loved Rory as if he were his own son."

"Perhaps he did," Rand said. "But it didn't stop him from sacrificing Rory when it came to a choice between his convictions and the boy's life." He smiled bitterly. "Tell me, O'Shea, did it increase your stature with your terrorist friends, when you handed them an eighteen-year-old martyr to use in their propaganda?"

Sheena expected her uncle to explode with rage, but she was surprised to see that he, too, was coolly controlled, his gray eyes narrowed and calculating. "You're intimating that I'm a member of the NCI?" he asked colorlessly. "That's as foolish as your other slander, Challon."

"You've been a member of the NCI for at least eight years, O'Shea," Rand said flatly. "Possibly longer. Your coffeehouse in Ballycraigh was used as a meeting place and as a storage warehouse for arms before you sold it four years ago. It was a very valuable asset. I'm quite surprised that they allowed you to sell it. But then, Sheena was potentially an even greater weapon, wasn't she?"

"None of this is true, Rand!" Sheena cried desperately. "Even that government man said that Uncle Donal had been thoroughly investigated and that he had no connection with the NCI. Can't you see how mistaken you are?"

Challon gave her a pitying glance. "There's no mistake, Sheena. Donal O'Shea's cover was almost perfect. It had to be, or he wouldn't have been of any use to them."

"Yet, you claim to possess knowledge, not even known to the authorities," O'Shea scoffed. "May I ask how you came by such information?"

"Money," Rand said simply. "You'd be amazed at how much information unlimited funds can buy. The private detectives I had investigating Sheena and her associates were most thorough." His gaze traveled to where Sean Reilly stood behind O'Shea. "For instance, there was the interesting tidbit regarding your charming associate. Reilly has been a member of the NCI since he was a kid of fourteen. He was setting off bombs in supermarkets by the time he was sixteen. It was something of a promotion for him to be selected as your assistant, wasn't it, O'Shea? What was the plan? Was he eventually to take over as Sheena's controller?"

Sheena shook her head dazedly. What Rand was saying was completely unbelievable. There was no way that Uncle Donal could be the monster he was describing. Not the man who had shown her both strength and affection since she was a small child. There must be some horrible mistake.

"No, it can't be true," she whispered.

"Of course it's not true," O'Shea said adamantly, turning her face up to look directly into her eyes. His gray eyes were brilliant with unshed tears. "Believe me, Sheena, you and Rory were all the world to me. How could I do such a thing?"

"Don't listen to him," Rand said desperately, his face taut and haggard. "For God's sake, believe me. Trust me."

"Come with me to Houston, Sheena," O'Shea said.

"We'll talk and get everything straightened out in your mind."

God, how she needed that, Sheena thought desperately. She felt as if she were being torn apart. She not only couldn't think, but she was beginning to be overcome by an odd lassitude that was paralyzing her emotions.

"Yes," she said vaguely. "Yes, I'll come."

"Sheena!" Rand's exclamation was both a rejection and a cry of pain.

She turned to him, her dark eyes almost blank with shock and agony. "I have to go, Rand," she explained numbly. "Please understand, I have to talk to my uncle." She turned away like a sleepwalker and walked toward the Datsun.

Sean Reilly was there ahead of her, swiftly opening the rear passenger door. She was about to step into the car when Rand appeared at her elbow. His expression was full of torment as he looked down into her pale, pain-racked face.

"Oh God, I'm sorry, love," Rand said raggedly, as he touched her cheek gently with one finger. "I know what hell this has put you through. Believe me, if there had been any other way, I would have taken it."

Sheena nodded, not looking at him. "I understand," she said, and somewhere down beneath the ice that covered her emotions she did understand. She got silently into the car, her eyes fixed straight ahead. If she didn't look at him, if she didn't speak, perhaps she'd be able to remain in this gray limbo.

She heard Rand curse, and then he leaned forward into the car to kiss her gently on the cheek. "I'm letting you go, Sheena," he said huskily. "I'll give you the time you need to get over the first shock, and then I'm coming after you."

"That wouldn't be wise, Mr. Challon." There was a touch of steel in Sean Reilly's usually silky voice. "We won't be caught off guard a second time. I'd advise you to keep your distance."

O'Shea entered the car by the other passenger door

and settled himself comfortably by Sheena, taking one of her cold, lifeless hands in both of his. "Sean is right, Challon," he said softly. "You won't be welcome around my niece in the future. It might even prove dangerous."

Rand straightened slowly, his face hardening to brutal ruthlessness. "I doubt that. Did I forget to mention that all of those investigative reports have been well documented and are locked up nice and tidy in a safe deposit box? You'd better hope that I stay healthy for a long, long time."

Sheena heard Reilly give a muttered curse as he slammed the door shut and then strode around the hood of the car to the driver's seat. It was only a moment later that the car lurched swiftly into motion, tearing away from the house and leaving Challon to gaze after them, his face a mask of grim implacability.

O'Shea leaned forward to speak to Reilly as they reached the rutted dirt access road. "Circle around as if we were heading for the highway," he said tersely. "Challon gave in a little too easily. It won't hurt to lay a false trail in case he decides to try to take her back."

"Right." Reilly nodded briskly, then proceeded to follow O'Shea's instructions.

O'Shea leaned back in his seat, his hand clasping Sheena's in a warm, comforting grip. His cool gray eyes were searching as they fixed on Sheena's blank, remote face. "You've made the right decision, lass. You know in your heart where you belong. Challon couldn't understand you as I do. We've been together a long time, haven't we, Sheena?"

Sheena nodded mechanically. "Yes, a long time."

So many years. She had a fleeting memory of the day that her uncle had taken Rory and her to the fair on the outskirts of Ballycraigh. Rory had been only fifteen then, she thought dazedly. She remembered how his face had lit up with pride when he had rung the bell with one powerful stroke of the massive hammer at the Test Your Strength booth. Uncle Donal had laughed and clapped him on the shoulder, fond pride on his face as well. So many years. She felt a melting of the ice around her heart as an aching pain pierced through her.

"It will be just as it used to be," O'Shea said complacently. "We'll forget this incident ever took place." He chucked her under the chin gently. "It never would have happened if I hadn't been such a thickheaded Irishman and not noticed how exhausted you were. You would never have let that playboy tycoon get around you if you'd been yourself."

She wondered what her uncle would say if he knew just how Rand had gotten around her. He evidently thought that Challon had used that devastating charm to beguile her into going off with him on a romantic interlude. Not that he probably wouldn't have succeeded if he'd had the time to use that particular weapon, she thought tenderly. It had taken him less than three weeks to make her fall in love with him and to become the center of her universe. A magical flood of memories of their time together flowed over her, melting the remainder of the shock that encased her. What was she doing here? she wondered wildly. Why was she sitting in this car speeding away from the only place she ever wanted to be, at Rand Challon's side?

"Ah, you're feeling better," O'Shea said gently, his eyes on the color coming back to her cheeks. "That's good, darlin'. Soon you'll be your old self. You shouldn't have let that man upset you so. You know that I would never use you as he said. You're my own colleen, just as you've always been."

"Yes, I'm feeling much better," Sheena said quietly.

Trust me, Rand had said. But if she trusted him, then she must believe what he had told her. How could she do that when she knew how her uncle had loved Rory? He would have to be a ruthless fanatic to sacrifice a boy he loved like a son on the altar of a political cause. But the members of the NCI were such fanatics, she realized bewilderedly. Oh, God, she didn't know what to think!

A frown on his face, O'Shea looked down at the small hand clasped in his. "These American's don't understand us, Sheena," he said, as if talking to himself. "They don't realize what it is to live in a country torn apart like our own is. How could they realize what we've suffered and what we must give up to preserve our heritage?" His bulldog face convulsed into a mask of pain, his icy gray eyes misting. "God, how I loved that lad."

Sheena went still, the breath leaving her body. No, it couldn't be true. She didn't want to hear any more.

"Rory was everything to me," O'Shea said hoarsely. "He was the finest lad that ever lived. Strong and brave and true." His gray eyes blazed with feeling. "Lord I was proud of that boy!"

Sheena closed her eyes, as a surge of sheer agony went through her. "Uncle Donal is proud of me," Rory had said. She had misunderstood. She had thought that her uncle had given Rory the same false assurance that she had in order to make his last hours easier, but that hadn't been it at all. It had all been true. Everything that Rand had said was the God's truth, and for a moment she didn't see how she could bear it.

"But there I go upsetting you again," O'Shea said, with false heartiness as he looked up to see her face white with misery. "You're a good girl to put up with an old man's maundering when you have your own cross to bear."

His last phrase inevitably brought to mind what Rand had said about O'Shea sending her on stage to be crucified. It all seemed so clear now. What had made the whole concept so unbelievable was her uncle's love for Rory. She couldn't conceive of a fanaticism so extreme that it could take perverse joy in sacrificing the object nearest one's heart. Yet now she had no doubt that her uncle had done just that. She would probably never know whether O'Shea had actually instigated that hunger strike, but it was almost certain that he had not tried to dissuade Rory when the others had given it up. Sheena gave a shiver of revulsion as she realized how many years of indoctrination and carefully spread poison had resulted in that horrifying night in Ballycraigh.

"We'll get you back to New York as soon as possible," her uncle said comfortingly. "You can stay in bed and relax all day tomorrow. You only have three numbers scheduled for your part of the benefit the next evening, so you won't even have to rehearse."

Three numbers. " 'Rory's Song'?" Sheena asked, knowing the answer before O'Shea nodded. One of the numbers would have to be "Rory's Song" if the pieces were to fit into the puzzle. So she was to be the instrument of O'Shea's fanatical passion just as Rory had been. Suddenly Sheena felt deluged by an icy rage that banished all the pain and confusion and filled her with a strength and confidence she had never known. No, by God, she would never let him use either her or Rory's death ever again!

O'Shea had leaned forward and was speaking to Reilly. "You can radio the helicopter now, Sean. Drive directly to Challon's private landing strip."

"Right you are, Donal," Reilly replied, picking up a receiver from under the dashboard and obeying his superior with the swift alacrity that always distinguished him. A ground-to-air radio, Sheena thought bitterly. She felt as if she were in the middle of a James Bond film.

"Helicopter?" she asked carefully, casually withdrawing her hand from O'Shea's. She felt physically ill at his touch.

O'Shea nodded. "We've had a helicopter standing by. We'll leave the car at the landing strip and board the 'copter there." His lips twisted in a smile of smug satisfaction. "We'll be out of here before Challon even knows about the landing. Then we'll transfer to a commercial jet at Houston Intercontinental."

"I see," Sheena said. "I thought we were just going as far as Houston tonight."

O'Shea smiled easily. "There's no reason for laying over now that you've come to your senses. We might just as well fly through to New York." He patted her cheek gently, a trace of triumph in his face. "You do want to come with us now, don't you, lass?"

He was so sure that he had won. He thought he had the strings of his little puppet securely in his own hands again.

"Yes, Uncle Donal," she said quietly, her dark gaze sure and steady as it met his. "I want to go to New York with you very much, indeed."

Night had fallen when they reached Challon's landing strip, but the field was brilliantly illuminated by the floodlights, and the scarlet helicopter that was just descending was experiencing no difficulties. The unauthorized landing, however, had brought a stream of mechanics and security personnel hurrying out on the tarmac from the concrete building beside the hangar.

"We'd better be prepared to do some fast talking," her uncle murmured to Reilly, as he helped Sheena from the car.

"It may take a trifle more than that," Sean answered silkily, a touch of the tiger in his gleaming smile. Why had she never seen past that polite facade? Sheena wondered. There was whip-cord tension and a sleek menace in Reilly's every move.

"None of that, Sean," O'Shea said sharply, glancing at Sheena's composed face uneasily. "Let me handle it."

They walked quickly across the runway, O'Shea and Reilly on either side of Sheena.

"Good Lord, Sheena, you're a busy little girl today. Does Rand know about this little adventure?" Nick O'Brien drawled, as he strolled lazily toward her across the field.

Sheena could feel the men on either side of her tense with the coiled danger of cats about to spring. O'Brien must have sensed the silent menace, for his own stance took on a subtle threat.

Sheena moved forward hurriedly a few paces to face O'Brien and try to avoid the dangerous confrontation that was festering in that silence. "Rand knows that I'm leaving, Nick," she said rapidly, her dark eyes frantically signaling a warning. "We've just left him." She forced a laugh. "I didn't think I'd see you again today. I thought you'd returned to Crescent Creek. What are you doing down here?"

"There's always a big poker game over here on Wednesday nights," he replied, his thoughtful gaze going past her to where O'Shea and Reilly were standing. "Isn't your departure a bit unexpected?" he asked quietly. "You're sure Rand knows that you're leaving?"

Sheena nodded. "Believe me, Nick, Rand knows that I've left for New York," she said earnestly. This conversation was bound to be repeated immediately to Rand. The reference to New York would eliminate any wild-goose chase to Houston. She heard O'Shea mutter something behind her, and she smiled grimly. He would almost certainly think the information had been dropped in all innocence. O'Shea's meek, docile puppet would never have the initiative to cause an upset in his plans.

O'Brien's searching gaze studied her face a long moment. "I still don't understand why he's letting you go, but it's not my place to try to stop you," he said slowly. "It's a bit of a puzzle."

She smiled brightly. "And I know how you love puzzles, Nick. I've been working on one myself lately, and suddenly all the pieces just fell into place."

"Really," Nick said, his eyes narrowing on her face. "That must have been very satisfying."

"Well, I had some help," she said softly. "Rand's a great one at solving puzzles, too, you know."

"No, I didn't know," O'Brien said thoughtfully. "I'm glad he was able to help you with this one."

"Sheena, love, it's time we were leaving," O'Shea said smoothly, as he joined her. "You'll have to chat with your friend some other time."

"I'm ready, Uncle Donal," Sheena said quietly, as she

turned back to O'Brien. "Goodbye, Nick, I hope I'll see you again soon."

"You're sure this is what you want, Sheena?" Nick asked soberly. "Sometimes when you walk away, it's damn hard to come back."

"I'm sure," she said quietly, her gaze fixed meaningfully on his lean, perplexed face. "It's always hard to break free of a cocoon, but it's necessary if a person is to reach one's full potential. I'm out of the cocoon now, Nick, and I definitely want to go to New York and do this concert."

"Of course you do," O'Shea said, his eyes gleaming with satisfaction. "But we must be on our way if we're to make our connection in Houston."

Sheena gave O'Brien a flashing smile. "I'll be seeing you, Nick," she said lightly, and turned away. A few minutes later she was being assisted into the scarlet helicopter, and the heavy metal doors slammed shut behind her.

Ten

Sheena added a touch of mauve shadow to her lids, which caused her eyes to appear even darker in their frame of black lashes, then gazed at her face objectively in the dressing room mirror. For a minute she considered using a touch of rouge but then decided against it. She had more than enough color in her cheeks that night. In fact, she had never looked more vibrantly alive in all her life.

There was a soft knock at the door, and at her invitation to enter, Donal O'Shea came in and closed the door behind him. "It's a very good house tonight, darlin'," he said easily as he came forward to stand behind her. He rested his hands lightly on her shoulders. "Very responsive for a benefit audience. It's unusual to see people who are paying fifty dollars a ticket so uncritical." He scowled in disgust. "They even applauded that young rock star who was just on."

Sheena smiled and reached for her rose pink lipstick, which she began applying carefully.

As her uncle observed her, a frown gradually clouded his face. "I'm not sure that gown suits you. Why didn't you wear one of your usual costumes? This performance isn't so outlandishly important that you had to run out yesterday and buy a new gown."

"I disagree. I think this performance is very important." She looked down at the black taffeta she was wearing. "I thought sure that you'd approve of my taste, Uncle Donal. It *is* black, and really quite dramatic-looking, don't you think?"

The garment in question looked more like a chic Chinese robe than a gown. Its loose flowing lines completely enveloped her small figure, from the high, stand-up collar to her feet, and the sleeves were long and lavishly full. The only decorations on the robe were the three large, shiny onyx buttons that fastened it, one at the throat, one at the waist, and the last at her knees.

"It's a bit too sophisticated for you, Sheena," he said, still frowning. "Next time I'll go along with you and help you choose." He dropped his hands from her shoulders and crossed to the gray velvet wing chair in the corner of the room. "Well, it's too late now to worry about it. You're on next."

Sheena nodded as she picked up a comb and began to tidy her glossy, dark curls. "I'll be ready," she said quietly.

O'Shea watched her silently for a moment, his gray eyes apparently puzzled by the expression on the thin, fragile face reflected in the mirror. "You've changed," he said abruptly. "You would never have wanted to choose your costumes before that blackguard, Challon, got hold of you."

Sheena smiled. "We all have to change as we grow older, Uncle Donal. I thought it was time I accepted some of the responsibility for my career myself. I've left the entire burden on you for much too long."

"Nonsense," O'Shea said gruffly. "I enjoy doing things for you. Just leave it to me from now on."

She didn't answer, and after a short silence, O'Shea asked suddenly, "You're not upset that I've scheduled you to do 'Rory's Song' tonight?"

Sheena shook her head. "Of course not," she said serenely. "I agree that it's entirely appropriate for me to sing it tonight. I might even have asked you to put it in if you'd omitted it."

"I'm glad you feel that way, Sheena," he said slowly. He rose to his feet and came forward to stand behind her once again. One hand reached out to touch her hair caressingly. "It's good to know you haven't forgotten how important it is." He picked up one curl and unwound it, only to release it to spring back into its former coiled tightness. "Rory loved your hair," he said absently, his eyes on her face. "Remember how he used to laugh when he did that?"

Sheena felt a sudden thrust of agony, and she closed her eyes swiftly to hide the pain and rage that was blazing out of them. Was she too calm and composed for him, then, that he must stir up that poignant memory?

"Yes, I remember," she said softly. Dark, laughing eyes that danced and teased and loved life with a wild zest. "I remember."

She opened her eyes and surprised a tiny glint of satisfaction in O'Shea's gray eyes, before it was quickly replaced by affectionate sympathy. "What a fool I am upsetting you right before you go on stage," he said, making a face. "You're an angel from heaven to put up with my clumsiness." He turned and walked toward the door, then paused there for a moment. "I know you're going to make me proud of you tonight, Sheena." The door closed softly behind him.

Sheena sat quite still for a long moment, fighting for control. She would not be overcome by these memories that would rip her composure to shreds. She must retain her strength of purpose if she was to survive this evening and come out victorious. She took several deep breaths, and gradually her serenity returned. By the time the knock sounded on the door to summon her to the wings, her face was as cool and composed as before O'Shea had entered the dressing room.

Sean Reilly was standing by O'Shea in the wings. "You look very elegant tonight, Sheena," he said, his smile flashing warmly. He handed her guitar to her, his eyes going over her lingeringly. "Quite the sophisticated young lady."

"Too sophisticated," her uncle said sourly. "Not the look we want at all."

"Thank you, Sean," Sheena said. "I'm sorry Uncle Donal doesn't agree with you." Her eyes were on the world-famous pianist on stage, who was taking her final bows.

"Perhaps it is a little unsuitable for your particular style," Reilly said smoothly, reversing himself as she knew he would. "But charming nevertheless."

The pianist had left the stage now, and O'Shea turned to Sheena. "You know what you're to do now?" he asked tersely. "First the two ballads and then 'Rory's Song.' "

"I know what the program calls for, Uncle Donal." The television talk show host, who was the master of ceremonies, was introducing her now, and she only had time to add softly, "Don't worry. I think you'll find this a very memorable performance." Her uncle was staring at her in uneasy curiosity as she walked slowly on stage to be greeted by an enthusiastic wave of applause.

Her uncle was right, it was a good audience, Sheena thought remotely, as she stood quietly center stage, waiting for the acclaim to subside.

When the huge auditorium was quiet, she spoke softly. "I'd like to beg your indulgence tonight. I'm going to change the program a bit, and I hope you won't be disappointed. I'd also appreciate it if you would refrain from any applause until I leave the stage."

Ignoring the surprised murmur that swept through the audience, she turned and walked swiftly to her stool, settled herself comfortably, and struck the first opening chords on her guitar. " 'Rory's Song,' " she announced in a low, sweet voice.

" *'As he lay dying, my Rory asked me why.*
I could find no answer, though God knows I tried.' "

As always when she sang the poignant notes, she was caught up in the sheer emotional impact of her memories, but this time she blanked out that night-mare recollection of Rory's death and tried to remember only the good things. Rory's smile and gay laughter, the time when they were small and he'd brought home the squirrel with the broken leg and nursed it all winter until it was well.

Gradually it became easier, and all the days filled with love and laughter flooded back to her. Rory had laughed so hard that he'd nearly fallen out of his chair when he'd put that rubber spider in her soup. Then when she had gotten so upset that she'd cried, he'd insisted on giving her his own soup, along with his dessert. The past enfolded her and almost all the memories were sweet and good. Why hadn't she realized that?

The last throbbing chords echoed through the auditorium with a wild, sad sweetness that was completely without bitterness. There were no tears on Sheena's cheeks, but her dark eyes were brilliant with tenderness and nostalgia as she sat silent for a long moment staring blankly ahead of her into the darkness. The dropping of a pin could have been heard, so silent was the auditorium, and Sheena was vaguely conscious that her audience was sharing, even helping in what she was attempting to do.

She closed her eyes for a brief instant, her throat aching with tears. Her voice was a mere breath of sound, but every person in the audience heard. They felt their own eyes mist with feeling. "Goodbye, Rory, love," she said huskily. "I'll miss you."

There was another long silence, and then Sheena slowly opened her eyes. Agony and regret no longer shone out of her face. They had been replaced by a strange serenity and the indomitable strength that O'Shea had noticed earlier. She spoke in a soft conversational tone, as if she were speaking to a roomful of friends. "That's the last time I'll ever sing 'Rory's Song,'" she said. "Thank you for helping me to say goodbye." She looked out into the darkness, her face earnest as a child who was trying to make the grown-ups understand what appeared so simple to her. "You see, it's time to put mourning aside and say farewell." She stood up slowly and put her guitar on the stool. "Someone once told me that life should be a celebration. It can't be that if we cling to the old wounds and the old strifes. We must let them go." Her hands were at the onyx buttons of her gown as she spoke, and she shrugged out of its heavy, dark folds as she ended simply, "As I have done."

She could hear the sharply indrawn breath of the audience and the swelling murmur that broke from them, but she ignored it serenely as she dropped the robe on the stool and came forward to stand in the center of the stage.

The brilliant scarlet chiffon gown she had worn beneath the black Chinese robe had been chosen very deliberately to convey a message as explicit as her words. Its cut was beautifully simple with a high empire waist and a slim, flowing skirt that barely suggested the curves it concealed. Her throat and upper breasts were left completely bare, and there were two long scarlet chiffon streamers at each shoulder that floated out behind her bannerlike, in a bold, gay challenge.

She stood quite still until the auditorium was silent once again, her small form straight and proud in its valiant plumage. "Now I'd like to sing you a song that I've just written about that celebration," she said, smiling gently and tossing back her black curls to reveal tiny golden loop earrings.

With no musical accompaniment, her throaty voice

rang out the simple, moving lyrics that built from soft, wistful entreaty to an exultant paean of triumph and hope.

> *"Have you heard the joyous whisper*
> *as it sweeps across the land?*
> *Have you seen the triumph*
> *in my Rory's eyes?*
> *Have you read the message*
> *that is written on the sand?*
> *And listened to his laughter like a song?*
>
> *Then you know that it is love*
> *that lifts our hearts.*
> *And you know that it is joy*
> *that sets us free.*
> *You know that there can be no death*
> *while memory remains.*
> *And if we stand together there's*
> *a place for you and me.*
>
> *It started as a whisper, but*
> *it soon will be a roar.*
> *From every hill and valley*
> *rings the call.*
> *Stop the killing, stop the hunger.*
> *Let peace pervade the earth.*
> *Give us love! Give us joy!*
> *Give us life!"*

As the last vibrant cry soared out over the rapt audience, Sheena felt almost dizzy with the heady exhilaration that was running through her veins. Oh, God, yes, this is what she wanted to say! This was what Rand had been trying to teach her. This was the only explanation for life that made any sense.

She stood there, her breasts heaving, her whole being electrified by the glorious, exciting *rightness* of the moment. Her dark eyes were blazing in a face that had the glow of a thousand candles as she gradually came back to earth.

Her lips parting in a smile of infinitely moving joyousness, she said simply, "Thank you for celebrating with me tonight," then turned and walked off the stage. She was conscious of neither the emotion-charged instant of silence, nor the almost hysterical burst of applause.

Her shoulders were immediately seized by a livid Donal O'Shea, and he was shaking her roughly. "You little fool, do you know what you've done?" he rasped furiously, his gray eyes narrowed to menacing slits. "You've spoiled everything!"

"Let her go, O'Shea," Rand Challon's tone was as deadly as a cobra's hiss. "I'll give you exactly three seconds."

Sheena looked past the glowering O'Shea and the equally furious Sean Reilly to where Rand stood a few feet away. She had been certain that he would be here, but she still felt a surge of gladness flow through her. His golden tawny coloring was set off beautifully by the black tuxedo he was wearing and he looked vibrantly magnetic and alive. Evidently her appreciation of his attractions was not shared by her uncle and Sean. Sheena saw both anger and apprehension in their faces as they turned to face Challon's taut figure.

"Stay out of this, Challon," O'Shea snarled furiously, his hands tightening on Sheena's shoulders. "This is all your doing!"

Challon shook his head. "You're wrong, O'Shea. You always have underestimated Sheena. It was her show from start to finish. Now let her go. She's leaving with me."

"The hell she is," O'Shea said. "She made a mistake tonight, but not one that can't be rectified. She stays here!"

"I said let her go," Challon said, and the menace had quadrupled in his voice.

"You'll find it difficult to take her." O'Shea's eyes narrowed. "There are two of us."

Reilly stepped a pace closer as if on cue.

"And there are two of us," Nick O'Brien said lazily, as he strolled out of the shadows. He, too, was dressed in evening clothes, and there was piercing menace in his aquamarine eyes.

There was a long moment of barbed silence as they confronted each other. Then O'Shea's grip gradually loosened on Sheena's shoulders. Sheena swiftly broke free of his hold and ran to Rand, to be enfolded protectively in the curve of his arm.

"There's no earthly sense to all this hullabaloo," O'Shea said easily. "There's obviously been a terrible misunderstanding. We've only to talk about it and get it straightened out." His coaxing gaze was fixed on Sheena's face. "Sheena, love, you know me. I've raised you like my daughter. You don't want to leave me now because of a parcel of arrant lies."

Sheena met his pleading gray eyes, and for a moment she was swayed, as he had intended, by the old affection and the bond of loyalty that he'd fostered in her. She shook her head as if to clear it, and immediately the memory of Rory's dark, bewildered eyes as he lay in that hospital room in Ballycraigh came to her.

Her face hardened into implacable bitterness. *"May you burn forever in hell, Donal O'Shea,"* she said softly. She turned and walked swiftly away.

Challon and O'Brien were immediately on either side of her, and Rand clasped her elbow in his warmly protective manner. "I couldn't have put it better myself," he said lightly. "You have a real way with words, Sheena."

"I'm glad that you approve," she said, smiling. "May I say that I was very glad to see you here tonight? I was afraid you might not understand my message."

"With Nick there to decipher all the nuances?" Rand scoffed. "It was mere child's play."

"It's wonderful to have one's genius appreciated," Nick said and grinned. "But I would have enjoyed it more if our Irish friends would have been more forth-coming. I was looking forward to a little excitement."

"When I filled him in on the set-up, he insisted on coming," Rand told Sheena. "I think he was anticipating a real honest-to-God shoot out."

"Well, one can only hope," O'Brien said wistfully.

Rand's golden eyes were glowing with a love and affection that caused Sheena's breath to catch in her throat. "Lord, I was proud of you tonight, dove," he said quietly. "You were the most magnificent thing I've ever seen in my entire life."

Sheena felt such a heady rush of happiness that there were no words to express it. She smiled at him with all the love in the universe in her face and said huskily, "Don't call me dove. Can't you see? I'm a lark!"

Rand looked at her face thoughtfully, before he smiled with a warm tenderness and pride. "Yes, I believe you are."

Sheena returned his smile with serene contentment and slipped her hand in his. She held her other hand out to Nick, and together the three walked out the stage door and into the night.

Fabulous
News
for
Iris Johansen
Fans!

From the spellbinding pen of this multi-talented author comes her most lush, dramatic, and emotionally touching romances yet—three magnificent love stories about characters whose lives have been touched by a legendary statue, the Wind Dancer.

ON SALE NEXT MONTH . . .

THE WIND DANCER

IRIS JOHANSEN has romance reviewers and noted romance writers raving about the advance copy they read of this thrilling historical romance!

A glorious antiquity, the Wind Dancer is a statue of a Pegasus that is encrusted with jewels . . . but whose worth is beyond the value of its precious stones, gold, and artistry. The Wind Dancer's origins are shrouded in the mists of time . . . and only a chosen few can leash its mysterious powers.

A magnificent love story, WIND DANCER is set in Renaissance Italy where intrigues were as intricate as carved cathedral doors and affairs of state were ruled by affairs of the bedchamber. This is the captivating tale of the lovely and indomitable slave Sanchia and the man who bought her on a back street in Florence. Passionate, powerful Lionello Andreas would love Sanchia and endanger her with equal wild abandon as he sought to win back the prize possession of his family, the Wind Dancer.

The Wind Dancer was born of a white-hot bolt of
    lightning.
So legend has it.

The Wind Dancer's worth was beyond price; its beauty
    beyond belief.
So legend has it.

The Wind Dancer could punish the evil, could reward
    the good.
So legend has it.

The Wind Dancer wielded the power to alter the
    destinies of men and nations.
So legend has it.

But legend, like history, can be distorted by time,
    robbed of truth by cynicism—
  yet be gifted with splendor by imagination.

In the following brief excerpt you'll see why *Romantic Times* said about Iris Johansen and THE WIND DANCER: "The formidable talent of Iris Johansen blazes into incandescent brilliance in this highly original, mesmerizing love story."

We join the story as the evil Caprino, who runs a ring of prostitutes and thieves in Florence, is forcing young heroine Sanchia to "audition" as a thief for the great *condottiere* Lionello who waits in the piazza with his friend Lorenzo, observing from a short distance.

"You're late." Caprino jerked Sanchia into the shadows of the arcade surrounding the piazza.

"It couldn't be helped," Sanchia said breathlessly. "There was an accident . . . and we didn't get finished until the hour tolled . . . and then I had to wait until Giovanni left to take the—"

Caprino silenced the flow of words with an impatient motion of his hand. "There he is." He nodded across the crowded piazza. "The big man in the wine-colored velvet cape listening to the storyteller."

Sanchia's gaze followed Caprino's to the man standing in front of the platform. He was more than big, he was a giant, she thought gloomily. The careless arrogance in the man's stance bespoke perfect confidence in his ability to deal with any circumstances and, if he caught her, he'd probably use his big strong hands to crush her head like a walnut. Well, she was too tired to worry about that now. It had been over thirty hours since she had slept. Perhaps it was just as well she was almost too exhausted to care what happened to her. Fear must not make her as clumsy as she had been yesterday. She was at least glad the giant appeared able to afford to lose a few ducats. The richness of his clothing indicated he must either be a great lord or a prosperous merchant.

"Go." Caprino gave her a little push out onto the piazza. "Now."

She pulled her shawl over her head to shadow her face and hurried toward the platform where a man was telling a story, accompanying himself on the lyre. A drop of rain struck her face; and she glanced up at the suddenly dark skies. Not yet, she thought with exasperation. If it started to rain in earnest the people crowding the piazza would run for shelter and she would have to follow the velvet-clad giant until he put himself into a situation that allowed her to make the snatch.

Another drop splashed her hand, and her anxious gaze flew to the giant. His attention was still fixed on the storyteller, but only the saints knew how long he would remain engrossed. This storyteller was not very good. Her pace quickened as she flowed like a shadow into the crowd surrounding the platform.

Garlic, Lion thought, as the odor assaulted his nostrils. Garlic, spoiled fish, and some other stench that smelled even fouler. He glanced around the crowd trying to identify the source of the smell. The people surrounding the platform were the same ones he had studied moments before, trying to search out Caprino's thief. The only new arrival was a thin woman dressed in a shabby gray gown, an equally ragged woolen shawl covering her head. She moved away from the edge of the crowd and started to hurry across the piazza. The stench faded with her departure and Lion drew a deep breath. *Dio*, luck was with him in this, at least. He was not at all pleased at being forced to stand in the rain waiting for Caprino to produce his master thief.

"It's done," Lorenzo muttered, suddenly at Lion's side. He had been watching from the far side of the crowd. Now he said more loudly, "As sweet a snatch as I've ever seen."

"What?" Frowning, Lion gazed at him. "There was no—" He broke off as he glanced down at his belt. The pouch was gone; only the severed cords remained in his belt. "Sweet Jesus." His gaze flew around the piazza. "Who?"

"The lovely madonna who looked like a beggar maid and smelled like a decaying corpse." Lorenzo nodded toward the arched arcade. "She disappeared behind that column, and I'll wager you'll find Caprino lurking there with her, counting your ducats."

Lion started toward the column. "A woman," he murmured. "I didn't expect a woman. How good is she?"

Lorenzo fell into step with him. "Very good."

Lion leaned back in his chair. His gaze went again to the smooth flesh of her shoulders. "And I like the shade of your skin. It reminds me of the gold of—" He stopped. He had been going to compare her to the Wind Dancer, he realized with a sense of shock. It must have been Lorenzo's remark that had brought the connection to mind. Possession. The Wind Dancer. Sanchia.

He lifted his goblet to his lips. "You know why you're here?"

"Yes." She moistened her lips with her tongue. "I knew when I saw you looking at me when I was in the bath. It's the same way Giovanni looked at my mother. You want to use my body."

The comparison irritated him. "I'm not Ballano," Lion said harshly.

"You had me bathed. You had me perfumed." She drew a quivering breath. "Do you want me to take off this gown and kneel on the floor now?"

"No!" The explosive rejection surprised him as much as it did her. "There are more pleasurable ways of taking a woman than if she were a bitch in heat."

"Yet the idea excited you," Sanchia said. "I saw that you were—"

"You see too much." A sudden thought struck him. "Are you trying to change my mind by comparing me to Ballano? Lorenzo said you use every weapon you possess."

"But I have no weapons here," she said simply. "I gave you my promise that I'd obey you."

No weapons. Lorenzo had said that, too, Lion recalled with frustration. She belonged to him. It was his right to use her body as he chose, with either tenderness or brutality. She knew this and accepted it. Why, then, was he feeling as if he had to make excuses for bedding her? "It doesn't have to be as it was with Ballano. I'll give you pleasure and—"

"No." Her eyes widened with bewilderment. "Why do you lie to me? It's always the man who has the pleasure. Women are merely vessels who accept them into their bodies and take their seed. Never once did my mother have pleasure."

"Because she was treated like an animal." Lion set the goblet down on the windowsill with a force that splashed the remaining wine on the polished wood. "I'll show you ways . . ." He stopped as he saw she was looking at him with complete disbelief.

He smiled with sudden recklessness. "Ah, a challenge. Shall I make you a promise, my doubting Sanchia? Suppose I tell you that I'll not use you as my 'vessel' until you beg me to do it. Until you're willing to kneel and let me use you as Giovanni did your mother because you yearn to have me inside you."

She looked at him in wonder. "Why should you make me a promise? You need not consider my feelings. I belong to you. It doesn't matter if I feel nothing when—"

"It matters to me." His tone held exasperation as well as barely concealed violence. "God knows why, but it does." He took her hand and pulled her to her knees before his chair. "And I'll probably regret that promise a thousand times before this is over. Now lift your head and look at me."

She obediently tilted back her head and she caught her breath at what she saw in his face. His eyes held dark, exotic mysteries and the curve of his lips was blatantly sensual.

"What do you see?"

"You want me."

"Yes." His big hands fell heavily on her slender shoulders. "And whenever I look at you from now on I'll be thinking of what I'd like to do to you." One callused hand released her shoulder and began to stroke her throat. Her skin was as velvet-soft as it lookea dn warm, so warm. . . . He felt hot lust tear through him, adding dimension to his manhood. "I'm going to touch you whenever I like." He slipped the material of the gown off her shoulders. "When it pleases me, I'll bare this pretty flesh and fondle you. No matter where we are. No matter who is watching."

She was gazing at him if mesmerized, the pulse fluttering wildly in the hollow of her throat.

"Are you a virgin?"

She moistened her lips with her tongue. "Yes."

"Good." He felt a primitive jolt of satisfaction so deep it almost obliterated the memory of Lorenzo's words.

■ ═══════════════════════════ ■

Just to whet your appetite even more, read what two of your favorite romance authors have to say about

THE WIND DANCER.

"IRIS JOHANSEN IS A BESTSELLING AUTHOR FOR THE BEST OF REASONS — SHE'S A WONDERFUL STORYTELLER. SANCHIA, LION, LORENZO, AND CATERINA WILL WRAP THEMSELVES AROUND YOUR HEART AND MOVE RIGHT IN. ENJOY, I DID!"

—Catherine Coulter,
New York Times bestselling
author of *Secret Song*

"SO COMPELLING, SO UNFORGETTABLE A PAGE TURNER, THIS ENTHRALLING TALE COULD HAVE BEEN WRITTEN ONLY BY IRIS JOHANSEN. I NEVER WANTED TO LEAVE THE WORLD SHE CREATED WITH SANCHIA AND LION AT ITS CENTER."

—Julie Garwood,
New York Times bestselling
author of *Guardian Angel*

■

ASK YOUR BOOKSELLER TO RESERVE A COPY OF THE WIND DANCER FOR YOU. IT GOES ON SALE IN THE BEGINNING OF JANUARY . . . AND READING IT IS THE ONLY WAY TO START OFF YOUR NEW YEAR!

The next engrossing book by Iris Johansen about those whose lives are enmeshed with the fate of the Wind Dancer is—

STORM WINDS

ON SALE IN MAY 1991

A glorious romance, STORM WINDS is set against all the turbulence and promise of the French Revolution. Clever and daring banker Jean Marc must retrieve the Wind Dancer from Marie Antoinette for his ill and aging father. Jean Marc's schemes lead him from the danger of Paris, to the tranquil gardens of southern France, to the perilous mountains of Spain. But soon his passion for the quest is overshadowed by his growing love for the one woman who can fulfill his dreams, the fiery artist Juliette.

A Must Read Romance!

THE LATEST IN BOOKS
AND AUDIO CASSETTES